The Mysterious Case
of the Allbright Academy

DIANE STANLEY

THE Mysterious Case OF THE Allbright Academy

HarperCollins*Publishers*

Library of Congress Cataloging-in-Publication Data
Stanley, Diane.
    The mysterious case of the Allbright Academy / Diane Stanley. — 1st ed.
        p.   cm.
    Summary: Eighth-grader Franny and her friends set out to find the
secret of their mysteriously perfect boarding school for gifted students.
    ISBN-13: 978-0-06-085817-9 (trade bdg.)
    ISBN-13: 978-0-06-085818-6 (lib. bdg.)
    [1. Boarding schools—Fiction. 2. Schools—Fiction. 3. Gifted
children—Fiction. 4. Behavior modification—Fiction. 5. Brainwashing—
Fiction. 6. Mystery and detective stories.] I. Title.
PZ7.S7869Mu 2008   2007010910
[Fic]—dc22   CIP
                                                                AC

Typography by Amy Ryan
1 2 3 4 5 6 7 8 9 10

First Edition

For my practically perfect children,
Catherine, Tamara, and John

The Mysterious Case
of the Allbright Academy

1

So there we were, all five of us, barreling down the road in the pitch-black dark, early on a Saturday morning. We were headed for the Allbright Academy, a school we'd never heard of till the week before, but which we hoped to attend in the fall.

Sounds crazy, I know. Looking back, I can't believe we ever thought it was a good idea. I guess we were just so dazzled by Martha Evergood's phone call that we simply lost our wits. (And yeah, I do mean *that* Martha Evergood, the first woman to be secretary of state and a genuine hero to every female on the planet.)

Dr. Evergood had been the guest speaker at a junior leadership conference that my sister, Zoë, went to in D.C. At the closing banquet they were seated at the same table, and Zoë proceeded to charm the socks off her, something Zoë has a natural tendency to do. Now, Dr. Evergood happened to be on the board of directors of the Allbright Academy, and Zoë struck her as a perfect candidate for the school. So Dr. Evergood picked up the phone and called their admissions people, urging them to get Zoë out there for testing ASAP.

The very next day the director of admissions called Mom and invited Zoë to apply. Apparently the invitation alone was a big deal. Allbright didn't let just *anybody* come out there to take the test—only very special students. And Mom shouldn't worry about expenses, either, he said. If Zoë was accepted, she would be on full scholarship!

Mom was really blown away by this, and clearly didn't know quite how to respond to it. Her end of the conversation started out kind of like this: "Oh . . . um . . . well . . . really? . . . Gosh!" Finally she got herself together and explained to the admissions guy that Zoë had a twin brother, J. D., as well as a big sister, Franny. (That's me, of course.) Mom doubted that Zoë would be willing to go to Allbright if she had to go without us.

No problem, the man said. We could come take the test too.

We were still deep in amazement over that call when the phone rang again. This time it was Dr. Evergood, herself, in person. Mom actually held her hand over her heart as she stood there listening to this very famous lady talk about how remarkable Zoë was and how Mom and Dad really ought to send her to this very special school. Allbright, Dr. Evergood explained, had been founded by two Nobel Prize–winning scientists for the specific purpose of developing the gifts of kids like Zoë, kids with special talents who would grow up to be our country's next generation of leaders.

"Please consider Allbright very seriously," Dr. Evergood said. "I think your daughter has enormous potential. She deserves the best education possible."

Really, after a sales pitch like that, how could we say no?

Now, I don't want you to think, from what I said earlier about losing our wits, that my family is totally nuts. I mean, yes, we were completely starstruck over Dr. Evergood's call. And, yes, we did make what seems like a pretty impulsive decision. But we did give the matter some thought first.

Mom and Dad said we were awfully young to be

going to boarding school, especially the twins. And we had always been public school people. But this was clearly an amazing, once-in-a-lifetime opportunity, and though they would miss us terribly, we could go if we wanted to. It was up to us.

We weren't sure we were ready to go to boarding school either. And besides, we had moved a lot over the years, because of Dad's job, and we were sick of changing schools. Under normal circumstances, we would have turned down Allbright's offer on the spot, no matter how many Nobel Prize winners had founded it.

But these weren't normal circumstances. It was almost as though fate had arranged for us to go to the Allbright Academy so we could discover the things that we did, and save the country from disaster. But I'm getting ahead of myself.

Let me just say that, only the week before, we had learned that the twins' school would be closing the following year, to be remodeled and turned into a high school. Zoë and J. D. would be going someplace new anyway. Then, the year after that, they would be moving a second time, to middle school. At least at Allbright they could stay in one place till it was time for them to go to college.

My situation was different. H. L. Mencken Middle School was brand-new and I would be staying there for three years. Unfortunately, my best (and I have to be honest here—only) friend, Beamer, would not. He was transferring to a special magnet program for the arts. So in a way, I'd be starting over again too, at least socially.

So those turned out to be the tipping points. Since Allbright was supposed to be so fantastic, why not start over there? Or at the very least, we ought to drive out to the school and check the place out.

The campus of the Allbright Academy is in a quiet, woodsy corner of Maryland, a two-and-a-half-hour drive from our house in Baltimore. Since we were supposed to be there by eight, we'd left home around five fifteen. That meant that we'd had to set our alarms for four fifteen, to allow time for all of us to shower, pack, and eat breakfast. Naturally, the twins and I went back to sleep as soon as we hit the road.

We pulled into the visitors' parking lot a little before eight. I had been dreaming that my above-mentioned friend, Beamer, was trapped on the roof of a school, which in my dream I knew to be the Allbright Academy, and which was on fire. I was frantic to save him. Then the engine stopped and I woke up.

Mom and Dad got out of the car. Wordlessly, Zoë and J. D. and I did the same. For about a minute we stood there in the parking lot, gaping speechlessly at the sight that lay before us.

I guess we were all expecting pretty much the same thing—a cluster of one-story redbrick flat-roofed buildings surrounded by playgrounds and parking lots. Since it was a boarding school, there would also be a couple of two-story redbrick dorms.

Instead, we were greeted by this unbelievably picturesque scene of broad lawns with trees and bushes and flowerbeds, with little paths winding through it, and a pretty big lake in the middle. Even this early in the spring, with the trees still bare, it was gorgeous.

The buildings *were* redbrick, but that's where the similarity ended. These looked historic, like maybe Thomas Jefferson had personally designed them. They had ivy growing up the walls and the roofs were shingled in slate. (I know this because Dad told us. He said slate was the top of the line, and very, very expensive.) As if the campus wasn't gorgeous enough already, it was set against the Blue Ridge Mountains, bathed in the warm pink glow of dawn.

"Yowza!" Dad said. "It's . . . it's . . ." Apparently struck speechless, he simply shook his head.

Mom removed the keys from his hand and opened the trunk so we could get our suitcases out. Zoë, J. D., and I would be spending Saturday night at the school, since their admissions testing took the better part of two days. I guess they wanted to make really, really sure we were smart enough to go there.

Rolling our bags behind us, we headed in silence toward the admissions building. There, waiting for us, was Allison, an Allbright senior who would be giving us a tour of the campus. It was mid-March, but it was cold that early in the morning, so she was bundled up in a white parka and ice-blue scarf. Shiny blonde hair cascaded out from under her matching ice-blue cap. She looked like she had stepped right out of a J. Crew catalog.

"Welcome to Allbright!" Allison said, displaying a set of perfect white teeth in an absolutely dazzling smile. I wondered whether her parents had spent a fortune on dentistry, or if she'd just hit the genetic jackpot. Understand: These were not just the usual straight teeth you get after putting up with years of braces—these were Hollywood teeth. Toothpaste-model teeth. I was weak with admiration.

"Is everybody warm enough?" Allison asked. "*Great!* Then let's get started. There's a lot to see and we need to get you back to admissions before nine."

We followed as she led us around the far side of the admissions building and down a gentle slope. "This is the living part of the campus," she explained, gesturing toward a cluster of large, elegant three-story buildings. "Each student is assigned to one of the cottages. That's where we live and eat our meals for the whole time we're at Allbright."

"Excuse me," Mom said. "Did you say *cottages*?"

"I know." Allison treated us to another stunning smile. "They don't look much like cottages, do they? I guess someone decided it sounded cozier than calling them dorms—but that's what they really are."

We were heading straight for one cottage in particular; probably the one where Allison lived.

"This looks more like a college than a prep school," Dad said.

"Well, yes. It was a college, once upon a time. Sort of a finishing school for girls. But it closed in the early seventies and Allbright bought the land and the buildings. The setting's gorgeous, isn't it? Great views! There are even hiking trails up in the hills over there. It's one of our PE options."

"What, hiking?" I asked. "You're kidding!"

"No, it's true. You can take all kinds of cool things—hiking or tennis or golf or swimming or mountain biking. We only do lifetime sports here, on the theory that people rarely play football or soccer after they leave school. We want to promote a healthy lifestyle for now and in the future."

Mom and Dad exchanged smiles of approval.

"Allbright was founded by scientists, as I'm sure you know. So they gave a lot of thought to health issues—wholesome food and plenty of exercise. Everyone here is extremely fit."

I studied the few Allbright students who were out and about that early in the morning, and saw that Allison was right. They were fit, every single one of them—fit and absolutely gorgeous. Not a single one was overweight or suffering from acne or cursed with bad hair. They had perfect posture. It was like being at cheerleading camp!

"This way," Allison said, leading us up a flight of flagstone steps to one of the cottages. There was a wooden sign over the entrance with incised lettering painted in gold. It said PRIMROSE COTTAGE. Allison smiled as she turned the knob on the big arched door. "Welcome to Primrose," she said, "my home away from home."

The front hall opened onto a large, beautiful room filled with couches and cozy armchairs. "This is our common room," Allison explained. "That's 'common' as in 'shared,' not 'common' as in 'falling below ordinary standards.'" Another smile. "It's our living room."

And no, it most definitely did *not* "fall below ordinary standards." Mom was positively bug-eyed, pointing out the carved oak paneling, the oriental rugs on the hardwood floors, the leaded glass in the windows, and the genuine, gold-framed art on the walls. Even the ceiling was decorated with fancy plaster designs. It was, without a doubt, the prettiest room I'd ever seen.

Even more astonishing was how clean and orderly everything was—and fifty or sixty kids lived there? Where were the sneaker marks on the upholstery? The coats and backpacks on the floor? The Coke cans and pizza boxes?

We saw none of these things, only three neat piles of newspapers on a big round table (the *Washington Post,* the *New York Times,* and the *Wall Street Journal,* in case you're wondering) and a handful of well-scrubbed teenagers reading them. They sat in chairs the way grown-ups do, without slouching and with both feet on the floor.

"Hi, Allison!" said a girl who looked to be about my age, lowering her copy of the *Post.* "Hi, visiting family!" she added, squinting her eyes in a cute way when she smiled. Like Allison, she was perky and adorable. We gave her a friendly wave, but there was no time for introductions. We had to keep moving.

"Down this hall is the dining room," Allison said, ushering us into a cavernous space with tall windows that looked like the room where the Knights of the Round Table used to eat on special occasions—except for the fact that the Primrose tables weren't round (they were long and narrow). And, of course, there was the buffet station at one end. But these minor factors aside, King Arthur would have felt right at home in the Primrose dining hall.

Breakfast was in full swing. Remarkably, everyone was eating (and apparently enjoying) what I can only describe as health food: oatmeal, whole wheat toast, grapefruit, yogurt, that kind of thing. No Froot Loops or Count Chocula to be seen anywhere.

"The food here is totally awesome," Allison said. "And very healthy. You'd be surprised how fast you lose your craving for junk food."

Mom and Dad exchanged more happy smiles.

Then we were on the move again, back to the common room and down a hall. Allison opened a door to reveal a sunny classroom full of desks.

"Study hall," she said. "It's required for grades six and seven, just to get them in the swing of things, but lots of eighth and ninth graders come, too. It's a good place to go if you really want to focus and get your work done. Plus, there are always teachers available to help with any questions or problems you might have. This is the girls' study hall. There's another one in the boys' wing."

Next door was a computer lab. We had just enough time to admire the huge collection of computers and printers and scanners before Allison herded us back toward the common room and up a flight of stairs.

"Everyone has a private room, but they're arranged in suites," she said. "Four rooms sharing a bathroom. A few of the seniors' suites have sitting rooms too, with fireplaces. They're awesome—something to hope for. I didn't get one, alas." She punctuated this with a pretend look of dismay, then smiled to show that she didn't really mind missing out on that fireplace. "And all the rooms have incredible closet space. My sister goes to Princeton now, and she never stops reminding me to *appreciate the closets*! It's like her mantra."

We climbed up another flight of stairs ("Great exercise for the legs!" Allison assured us), and then went down a hall and to the left. She stopped in front of Room 317, turned the knob, and ushered us in. "My humble abode," she said.

The room was smaller than mine at home, but it was lovely, with hardwood floors and two large leaded-glass windows looking out at the mountains. And maybe it was just because Allison knew she'd be leading a tour and bringing people by, but *her bed was made*—at 8:15 on a Saturday morning! Not only that, but apparently all her clothes were neatly hung up in the famous closet. Yes, in fact, they were! (Allison opened it proudly to show us.)

"*This*," said my mom, "is without a doubt the tidiest dorm room I have *ever* seen."

"Oh, well," Allison said, blushing cutely. "Company coming and all."

We peered into the spotless bathroom, where

Mom commented on the presence of a tub, apparently a rarity in dorms. Then we were heading back down the stairs, exercising our legs a little bit more.

"It's too bad we don't have time to visit *all* the cottages," Allison was saying. "Each one is a little different, and they have their own unique features, like darkrooms or language labs—depending on the specialty of the house."

"What do you mean, the specialty of the house?" Dad asked.

"Well, you know, the artsy kids live in Aster Cottage, and the techies are all in Sunflower. It's not official or anything, but it's pretty obvious."

"So, what kind of kids live in Primrose?" asked Zoë, who was clearly dying to live there. Then again, so was I. Who wouldn't?

"Well, we're not as easy to categorize, but I'd say we're mostly outgoing, organized types. Active in student government. In fact, I'd bet there hasn't been a student-council president in the history of Allbright who didn't live in Primrose. We're into politics and world affairs. Hence, the newspapers."

"But how do they know where to put you?" I asked. "I mean, how do they know you're a techie or an artist or a future politician?"

Allison laughed. "Trust me, they know everything about you. Or at least they will by Sunday afternoon, when they're done with the testing. Just you wait! They'll find out if you have perfect pitch or athletic talent or a gift for languages. They'll spot any learning disabilities you might have, they'll pinpoint your ideal learning style, and they'll know what professions would be best for you—even what college you should go to. It's what makes the school tick. It's what makes it possible for them to give each student an education that is perfectly tailored for him, or her."

"Specially tailored?" Mom asked, literally stopping in her tracks. "What do you mean, exactly?"

"Just that. If you're talented in math, you get an advanced math program and can progress at your own rate. You're not stuck in eighth-grade math just because you're in eighth grade. And if, say, you're a visual learner, they group you with other visual learners and your classes are taught with that learning style in mind. If you have deficits that show up in the testing, they give you help with them. And whatever special talents you have, they give you all sorts of amazing enrichment opportunities to develop them—field trips, mentors, summer internships, workshops."

"That is just positively beyond belief!" Mom said. I could tell that whatever doubts she had about sending us to Allbright had now completely vanished.

Allison shrugged and made an apologetic face. "It's true," she said. Then we were moving again.

"Um, Allison," Dad said. "Can I assume there are also some *adults* living here at Primrose?"

"Of course!" she said, laughing. "Every cottage has two 'Mum's' apartments—a girls' Mum and a boys' Mum. They're teachers, mostly, who live here on campus. Some are married couples, some are single. But they act as our advisers and counselors. They look after us, make sure we behave ourselves, dry our tears." She flashed another huge smile. "So we call them our Mums. Even the guys! Kind of silly, I guess."

She checked her watch. Obviously we were running slightly behind schedule, so we waved goodbye to the kids in the common room, who were still reading ("'Bye, Allison! 'Bye, visiting family!"), and hiked across campus to the academic area. There we toured the science building (with equipment sufficient to build a spaceship), the arts building (which included painting, sculpture, and ceramics studios, a film-editing room, and a drama wing with costume rooms, storage for sets and props, and a state-of-the-art theater), the gym (with a huge weight room, an indoor track, squash and tennis courts, and an Olympic-size pool), and the three-story library. There were several other general-purpose buildings, each named after a donor—Fisk Hall and

Harrington Hall, that kind of thing. These were where you went for your English classes and foreign languages and history, Allison said.

And then we were jogging aerobically back in the direction of the admissions building, Allison apologizing for rushing us but reminding us that we didn't want to be late for the testing. When we reached the door, panting a little from the effort, Allison squeezed Mom's and Dad's hands and hugged the twins and me. We thanked her and waved good-bye as she trotted away in the direction of Primrose.

We never saw Allison again after that (by the time we arrived at Allbright the following fall, she was already gone, putting up with small closets at Princeton). But I, for one, never forgot her. She was the perfect Allbright product: smart, beautiful, accomplished, and confident—all the things I longed to be. And I remember wondering if it was the school that had made her that way.

If I got in, would Allbright work its magic on me, too?

2

Allbright did its testing in October. Acceptance (or rejection) letters went out in January. But there were always special cases that popped up after that, kids like Zoë who had just been "discovered," or places opening up because a student moved or got sick or something like that. We were part of this later, much smaller, wave of applicants.

We were separated by grade for the testing, and as I split off from Zoë and J. D., it occurred to me (as it had so often before) how lucky they were, never having to go into scary new situations alone. They always had each other.

And this was definitely a scary situation. I had no idea if I could pass this marathon of tests, or even what kind of tests they would be. Allison had mentioned perfect pitch; would they ask me to sing? Athletic ability—would I have to walk on a balance beam or throw a ball? I generally did pretty well on standardized tests, but I had a hunch that I was not in the same league with the Allbright kids. Unfortunately, I had fallen in love with the school, and I really, really wanted to get in.

The meeting place for future eighth graders was a small waiting room, kind of like a fancy doctor's office, with nice pictures and expensive furniture, and a second, interior door at the back. Two kids were already there, sitting across from each other in silence, both of them reading.

One was a tall boy with curly pale blond hair. His lashes and brows were that same light color, and his face was pinky white. He was slouched in his chair, legs splayed out, deeply engrossed in a fat paperback. I'm sure he heard me come in, but he didn't bother to look up.

The other was a sporty-looking round-faced girl with curly dark hair pulled back in a ponytail. She had a magazine in her lap, though I realized when I looked at her again that she wasn't actually reading it. She was staring at her shoes in a dejected sort of way.

A couple of beats after I came in, she looked up and offered me a brave smile. I went over and sat down beside her.

"Hi," I said, "I'm Franny Sharp."

"Cal Fiorello," the girl said.

There followed the usual awkward moment of silence that I always hate. I'm not all that good at making small talk, at least with people I don't know. But I could tell that this girl needed someone to talk to. Since paleface across the way didn't seem interested, that was going to have to be me. I ran through a mental list of possible subjects.

"So, what do you think about all this testing?" I asked. "Weird, huh? I mean, *two whole days*? My dad says even for college they don't do that."

Cal's eyes sparkled with the threat of tears. "Yeah, I'm afraid it's going to be really hard," she said. "Being 'above average' isn't going to cut it. I just hope they need a forward for their field-hockey team. That's one thing I'm definitely good at."

"Uh," I said. I didn't want to send her over the edge, but on the other hand, I didn't want her to get her hopes up about the hockey thing. "I heard they don't have team sports here. Just stuff like tennis and golf. 'Lifetime' sports."

"Oh, great!" she said, her shoulders slumping. "That is *just great*."

Since we had clearly wandered onto sensitive ground, I decided to change the subject to something utterly bland and neutral, something that couldn't possibly upset anybody.

"So, where do you live?" I asked. "Baltimore? D.C.?"

That did it! Now the tears actually started to flow. And all I'd asked was where she lived. Cheez!

Cal pulled a Kleenex out of her pocket and dabbed at her eyes. "I'm sorry," she said. "I've got to pull myself together. You probably think I'm a nutcase."

"No," I said, "but you do seem kind of upset."

"Yeah," she admitted. "Sorry. It's just that when you asked where I lived—well, the fact is, I don't really live anywhere. My dad's in the Foreign Service, and so we've lived all over the world— Hong Kong, Jakarta, Colombo. I know you probably think that sounds really cool, but trust me—it's not easy starting over all the time in a new place with new people. You kind of lose the energy for it after a while."

"Actually," I said, laughing, "I know *all* about that, minus the exotic places. With us it was more like Cincinnati and Minneapolis and San Diego. I kid you not, for almost my whole life we've moved every single year. And yeah, it does get really old. My brother and sister and I actually went on strike to make Dad quit consulting and take a permanent job in Baltimore."

She nodded, then got that sad look again. "But,

see, you have a sister and a brother. And you probably have a mom, too," she said.

That took me aback a little. "Well, yeah," I said.

"All I have is my dad. And the last two years he was stationed in Sri Lanka, so I boarded at the American Embassy School in New Delhi. I only got to see him in the summer and on school vacations. That was bad enough, but *now* he's being transferred to Goristovia, and he says it isn't safe there . . ." She started sniffling and fished out her Kleenex again. "I'm sorry," she said. "You don't need to listen to all this."

"Yeah, I do. Quit apologizing."

"You're nice," she said. "Thanks. I'm not always like this, really." I reached over and patted her arm.

"So, anyway," she said, "last week Dad announces that he wants me to go here, because they have a summer program, and you can even stay here over Christmas break if you need to—and, well, I just totally lost it. I feel . . . I feel . . ." She took a deep, shuddering breath and buried her face in her hands.

Abandoned, I thought. Cheez Louise, what was her dad thinking? About his job, apparently, and not his kid.

I looked across at the pale-faced boy to see if he was listening. He was still hunched over his book—except that now he had this kind of irritated expression on his face, like our conversation was making it hard for him to concentrate.

Since I knew he wasn't looking, I stuck my tongue out at him. I found this strangely satisfying.

"What makes it even harder," Cal was saying, "is that this job is a promotion, a really big deal for him. And if he can't find some place to put me, then he'll have to turn it down. They'll probably give him some stupid paper-pushing job in D.C.—and this is a guy who speaks, like, *seven* languages. If his career is ruined, it'll be all my fault." She was crying again.

"Oh, Cal!" I said, and reached over and gave her a hug. She hugged me back, really hard. After about a minute of this, I could tell from her breathing that she was starting to calm down. Then, just before she let go, she whispered into my ear, "Is that kid staring at us?"

"No," I whispered back. "He's totally oblivious. A really good book, apparently."

"*Moby-Dick!*" she said, then leaned back and raised her eyebrows.

We locked gazes.

"No way!"

"Yes, way!"

It passed through my mind just then—okay, I know this sounds kind of mean—but I thought maybe he had brought that book along to impress the admissions people. I was busy wondering why I had taken such a sudden dislike to this kid—who was, after all, just minding his own business and enjoying his book—when the door opened and a fourth student came in.

He stopped in the middle of the room, just as I had done, and looked around to assess the situation. The pale one continued to act like he was the only person in the room, whereas Cal and I greeted him with friendly smiles. We were clearly his best bet.

He came over and sat down next to me, leaning forward so he could talk to Cal, too. "Hi," he said, "I'm Brooklyn—and yes, I was born there. Brooklyn Offloffalof."

I had no idea what was going through Cal's mind at that moment, but I, personally, was busy ordering myself not to stare. Brooklyn, you see, was drop-dead gorgeous, with caramel skin, hazel eyes, and a head full of literary dreadlocks. (In case you've never heard of literary dreadlocks—which I'm sure you haven't, since I made them up—they are the short kind, which I associate with writers and artists and filmmakers. The long kind I call Rasta dread-locks; they are for hippies and reggae singers. Both are subsets of my general theory of serious hair, which I will not bore you with right now except to say that Brooklyn's hair was plenty serious. You could easily picture him, in about fifteen years, as the coolest professor on the Harvard campus.)

"Anybody from the school show up yet?" he asked, unaware of the three-ring circus going on in my head.

"No." I checked my watch. "It's three minutes to nine."

"You nervous?" Cal asked, and I noted that, despite her mottled cheeks and bloodshot eyes, she now looked remarkably cheery.

Brooklyn shrugged.

"Not even a little bit?" I asked. "They're getting ready to test us within an inch of our lives!"

"True, it's excessive. But I figure, if they don't want me, then I shouldn't be here. I'm happy enough at the school where I am—though I think I'll probably get in. They invited me to apply."

"They *invited* you to apply?" Cal asked, astonished.

"He's being recruited," said a voice from across the room. "As am I."

The pale one had spoken!

Of course he had been listening to us all along, every single word, but he hadn't felt the need to say anything till now, when he had the chance to show off.

"Whoa!" Cal said, turning to me with a panicked look on her face. "Are you being recruited too?"

"Sorry, no," I answered. "I'm just an ordinary mortal." As soon as I said it, I knew I'd been rude, and I turned to Brooklyn to see if I'd offended him. I wasn't sure, but I didn't think I had.

Brooklyn has this way of looking at you that I can't exactly describe—and I've had plenty of time to think about it since then. He doesn't smile much—not the big toothy kind of smile anyway. He just gets this little amused curl around the corners of his mouth. At the same time, he looks you right in the eye in this calm, sure way. You feel like he can see inside you, all the way down to your bones. It's creepy, and thrilling, and very, very attractive.

"I'm sure you'll do fine," he said. "Both of you."

Was that a snicker I heard just then, coming from the other side of the room? Or was the pale one having sinus trouble? Judging from his downcast eyes and satisfied grin, his sinuses were just fine. I shot him a dirty look, which unfortunately he didn't notice.

Just then (at the stroke of nine), the rear door opened and a cute redhead in a blue suit came out, her heels making brisk, businesslike clicks on the tile floor. I was pleased to note that she had serious hair. I was surprised to note that she was carrying a plate of brownies.

"Morning, kids," she said, very chipper. "I'm Evelyn Lollyheart, assistant to the headmistress here at Allbright. But this weekend, I'm in charge of you rising eighth graders. I'll be getting you started on your tests. There'll be lots of to-ing and fro-ing over the next two days, so I'm sort of the traffic cop."

I was just thinking that she looked kind of like Agent Scully on *The X Files*, only maybe not quite that pretty, when she began offering the brownies around like some hostess out of a fifties sitcom.

The pale one shook his head. "No, thanks," he said.

"Oh, come on—Prescott, is it? I thought so. Really, you've got to try them. The brownies are an Allbright tradition." He reached out reluctantly and took one.

Then Ms. Lollyheart came over to us. "You must be Cal, right?" she said—and she actually *winked*! I kid you not.

"Oh!" Cal said, like she had suddenly gotten the point of some joke. "Hi!" And she flashed Ms. Lollyheart a huge smile.

I'm sure I wasn't the only person in the room who wondered what that was all about. Cal told us later that her dad and Evelyn Lollyheart had been friends back in their college days. Mr. Fiorello had recently gone to his twentieth reunion, where they ran into each other. She started telling him about this amazing school where she worked, and she made it sound so great that he started asking her more and more questions, hoping that Allbright would turn out to be the perfect place to dump his daughter while he went off to Goristovia to encourage democracy and try to avoid getting blown up.

"Believe it or not," Ms. Lollyheart said, "the brownies are actually healthy. Chock full of vitamins and minerals and fiber and antioxidants. No sugar, of course. Dr. Gallow's special recipe, the crown jewel of Allbright's nutrition program. We always welcome new students with the brownies. And you're Franny, right? And Brooklyn, of course."

We all agreed that the brownies were delicious— even Prescott, who despite his original reluctance had scarfed his down and was now licking his fingers. And really, who could possibly resist a brownie at nine in the morning?

3

New-student orientation began on a Monday, and the returning students wouldn't arrive till Saturday. That gave us five days to settle in and bond with our fellow newcomers.

Monday morning, after we'd said good-bye to our parents, we all gathered in Willard Theater for the welcoming speeches. Zoë, J. D., and I sat together, but I kept a watchful eye out for Brooklyn (who I felt sure would have been accepted), and Cal (for whom I was keeping my fingers crossed).

At exactly nine—they're always very prompt at Allbright—a woman walked out onstage. She was tall—about six feet two in her spike heels—and slim and blonde. She could have been a high-fashion model, except that she didn't have that starved, bored look you always see in the magazines. This woman, you could tell just by looking at her, was an important person. Everything about her was elegant and serious, from her slicked-back hair to her perfect manicure and her conservative pearl-gray suit.

She wished us good morning in a deep, velvety voice that reminded me of Ingrid Bergman's in *Casablanca*. After we pledged our allegiance to the enormous flag at the front of the room and sang the national anthem, we all sat down and the meeting got started.

"I am Dr. Katrina Bodempfedder," the beautiful lady said, "headmistress at Allbright, and it's my great pleasure to welcome you here today." She flashed a broad smile. Even from that distance I could tell that, like Allison, she had perfectly beautiful teeth. "And what an extraordinary group of young people you are! Over the next few months, as you get to know one another better, you will discover what I already know from reading your test results: that there is enough brainpower in this room to light up Las Vegas. Your talents are varied, but there is not a single person here who is not truly, extraordinarily gifted." She shook her head at the wonder of it.

Um, I thought. Not exactly true. I knew for an

absolute, dead-solid fact that there were at least *two* people in the room who were not "truly, extraordinarily gifted"—and I was one of them. The other was sitting beside me, carefully folding a small square of paper torn from a corner of his orientation program into a tiny origami crane: my little brother, J. D.

I might as well get this out of the way right now. After all that testing, neither of us was accepted by the Allbright Academy. They'd only wanted Zoë.

So, naturally, you're wondering why, if that was the case, all three of us were sitting there in Willard Theater at the opening of new-student orientation. Well, the answer is simple. As Mom had predicted, Zoë refused to go without us—and especially not without J. D.

They're twins, after all. Though complete opposites, personality-wise, they are very close. And Zoë is incredibly loyal to the people she loves. As far as she was concerned, either we all went or we all stayed home. And she wouldn't budge, either, no matter how hard we tried to convince her she was passing up an amazing opportunity. Finally, Mom called the school to say that Zoë had decided to decline.

That should have been the end of the story, except that Zoë must have tested off the charts in *something* (what, exactly, I can't imagine—unless it was in being adorable; Zoë has never been a top student), and they wanted her desperately. So desperately, in fact, that they took us, too—all on full scholarship.

This felt kind of icky to me at first, getting into a school that hadn't really wanted me, just because I was Zoë's sister. But it didn't bother J. D. in the slightest.

"Who cares how we got in?" he'd said. "It's a cool place. We'll all be together. Be glad about it." I'd decided to take his advice.

Dr. Bodempfedder folded her arms on the podium and leaned into the microphone. "And how fortunate," she continued, "that you remarkable young people have the opportunity to attend this equally remarkable school, a place where your talents will be cultivated and your aspirations can take wings."

Zoë was drinking this in with an expression of absolute rapture. I swear, when she gets that look on her face, she practically radiates light. J. D., on the other hand, was rolling his eyes and checking his shoulders for sprouting wings. I nudged him with my elbow.

"Be nice," I said. J. D. shrugged and went back to his origami.

"We owe enormous thanks to Dr. Linnaeus Planck and Dr. Horace Gallow, whose vision and dedication made it all possible. Both, as I'm sure you know, are recipients of the Nobel Prize—in physics and chemistry respectively—the highest honor a scientist can win. Yet I believe both Dr. Planck and Dr. Gallow would tell you that, of all they have accomplished in their illustrious careers, they are proudest of founding this school.

"Dr. Planck retired nearly twenty years ago, but he was always here on opening day to welcome the new batch of 'wonderlings.' Sadly, he's not well enough to do that anymore, and we miss his wit and wisdom here at Allbright. *However* . . ."—here she smiled to indicate a change of subject to something more upbeat—"Dr. Gallow is still very much with us. He continues to serve as the president of our board of directors and titular head of school. I don't say this just because he's my boss"—she paused here so we could laugh—"but he is one of the brightest, most dedicated human beings I have ever met. It is an honor for me to introduce him to you this morning. Dr. Gallow!"

Everybody clapped as a handsome gray-haired man came out onto the stage, shook Dr. Bodempfedder's hand, and took his place behind the podium.

"Good morning," he said, adjusting the microphone and pushing his glasses up on his nose. He gazed out at us in silence for a moment, taking in our collective wonderfulness, like Midas admiring his gold. Then he smiled very broadly and got started. (In case you're wondering, his teeth weren't quite as nice as Dr. B's, but they were pretty nice all the same.)

"It's always such a thrill for me to welcome new students on opening day," he said. "I know how much work went into bringing you here—a rigorous talent search on the part of our staff and board members, and an equally rigorous testing and admissions process for you." (A polite titter of laughter from the students.) "And the results, as always, are spectacular. The talent here in this room, the promise of greatness to come—well, it just blows me away!"

Those adjectives were really piling up thick, I thought: talented, brilliant, smart, incredible, bright, gifted, exceptional, amazing, extraordinary, spectacular. Cheez! There was no end to it! What hope was there for somebody like me, who could more aptly be described as average, ordinary, regular, typical, or normal? I wondered if J. D. was thinking the same thing. Maybe that was the reason for the origami—to take his mind off the sea of excellence we were nearly drowning in.

"There are, of course, plenty of other fine schools in this country," Dr. Gallow was saying. "They too attract bright students—some of them as bright as you—who will get into the top universities and professional schools, and then spend their lives working in well-paid, prestigious professions. But here at Allbright, we expect something greater from our graduates. We hope you will think beyond an easy life of wealth and success. We hope you will choose a life of service. When I look out at your young faces, I see more than just a room full of talented children. I see the future of this country.

"Today America leads the world—but it may not lead it much longer. Did you realize that forty-two nations have lower infant mortality rates than we do? We're forty-eighth in the world in life expectancy. Our high-school students score *below average,* worldwide, in math, science, and problem-solving skills. How long before we join all those other great countries—Egypt, Greece, Rome, Spain, England—who once led the world and then fell behind and became irrelevant? Will China or India soon surpass us, to become the new superpower? Not if I can help it! That's the very reason Dr. Planck and I founded this school—to find you, the best and the brightest young people in America, and prepare you to take your place in the ranks of this country's leaders. And when the torch is passed to you, be ready, be bold, be dedicated! Our future is in your hands!"

Wild applause.

J. D. tore off another tiny square and began methodically folding it into a pineapple.

4

After Dr. Gallow's rousing speech we were divided into groups by class. Zoë and J. D. stayed in the theater with the other sixth graders (they needed the space because sixth was the entering class and there were a lot of them). I headed for Wexler Hall, next door.

A tall man with a clipboard was waiting at the entrance. He checked off my name and pointed out the table of snacks against the far wall. Juice and brownies. Ah, yes—the famous Allbright brownies. I scurried over and took two.

I didn't recognize a soul. These kids had all tested in the fall, and though they knew one another from that weekend back in October, they were complete strangers to me. Unfortunately, I've never been able to walk up to people I don't know and strike up a conversation. So I was just standing there alone, feeling awkward and studying my brownies like an idiot, when I spotted Brooklyn, waving and heading in my direction. Relief washed over me.

"Franny!" he said, with a rare big smile. "Some speech, huh? We're the future of the nation."

"Very heavy stuff," I agreed.

Brooklyn was craning his neck, searching the crowd. "Have you seen Cal yet?"

"No," I said. "Do you know for sure she's here?"

"Yeah, I saw her name on the clipboard."

People were already moving into the meeting room. "Maybe she's inside," I said. "Let's go look."

Brooklyn suddenly grabbed my arm. "Hold on!" he said. "I see your favorite person!" I followed his gaze and saw Prescott, leaning against the wall, wearing his trademark look of sullen disdain.

I said, very softly, "Ooof! Ooof!" and Brooklyn replied, "Ooof! Ooof!"

It was our little joke from those two days of testing the previous spring. Brooklyn and Cal and I had formed this cozy little trio—which left Prescott out, of course. And we'd felt kind of guilty about that. Yeah, okay, he'd been arrogant and unpleasant at first, but maybe it was just social anxiety or something, your typical science-nerd awkwardness. So we actually tried to draw him in, to give him a chance to be part of the group. But he wasn't interested. He kept wandering off to be by himself, and when he was forced to be in the same room with us, he would pull out *Moby-Dick* or simply turn his back on us. Finally we just stopped trying and left him alone.

"What's *with* him, anyway?" Cal had asked at one point.

"He's very aloof," Brooklyn had said, drawing out the "oof" in a funny way. He liked the sound of it, apparently, because he said it again, "Ooof . . . ooof!"

"'Who let the dogs out?'" I couldn't resist. "'Ooof . . . ooof!'"

It had sort of taken on a life of its own. Whenever we saw him coming, at least one of us would start *oof*ing. I know it sounds mean, but trust me, he had definitely asked for it.

"Well, well!" Brooklyn said. "The gang's all here." And sure enough, there was Ms. Lollyheart.

"Ladies, gentlemen!" she hollered over the din. "Could you please take your seats now so we can get started?" Everyone put down juice glasses, finished their brownies, and made their way inside. Brooklyn and I sat near the back and continued our search for a dark, curly ponytail.

"Good morning!" The buzz quieted. "I'm Evelyn Lollyheart. You may remember me from your delightful two days of testing last year. For those who were too exhausted or too terrified to retain that information, I'm your all-purpose Allbright representative—by day, I'm assistant to the head-mistress, by night I'm the girls' Mum over at Larkspur Cottage. And this week I'll be your orientation leader.

"I'd like to begin by inviting each of you to come up and introduce yourself to your new classmates. We need you to keep your remarks pretty short so it doesn't take all day. Just tell us your name, where you're from, and a little about what makes you special.

"Now, so you won't think I'm picking on any-body, we'll do this alphabetically. You A and B peo-ple—you're used to this by now. You can handle it."

As it turned out, there weren't actually any A people, so the first to be called up was Prescott Bottomy III.

"Oooooooooooof!" whispered Brooklyn.

"Ooofity-oof," I whispered back.

Prescott got up from his seat in slow motion and strolled up to the dais—like there was no need to hurry, his time was *so* much more important than ours.

"Hi," he said, when he finally got up there, "I'm

Prescott, and I grew up in Boston. But my parents are on the Hopkins Med School faculty now, so we live in Baltimore. Roland Park, actually." (Well, of course! Important to let us know that he lives in a ritzy part of town.) "My father is a hematologist/oncologist, and my mother is a cell biologist.

"Not surprisingly, I'm strong in science and math. I came in second in the National Math Exam last year. I'm also extremely good with computers. Actually, if we're being honest here—*are* we being honest here, Ms. Lollyheart?"

Ms. Lollyheart said that we were.

"Actually, I do well in the humanities and languages, too—pretty much across the board, grades-wise and testing-wise. I came in third in the National Latin Exam, for example."

I expected Brooklyn to go "Ooof" again, but he didn't. He was staring up at the podium with that penetrating gaze of his, clearly amazed by Prescott's arrogance and the cluelessness he showed in expressing it so bluntly. Like Frankenstein's monster, you really had to wonder what had made him the way he was.

"Got any plans for the future, Prescott?" Ms. Lollyheart asked. "Will you be following your parents into the medical field?"

"Something like that, though I'd rather do research than treat patients."

"Well, I think you'll be pleased with the level of science we teach here. You will be matched with a mentor—all of you will have mentors—someone who is doing high-caliber research, quite possibly at Hopkins. You'll also have the opportunity to do summer internships at medical labs. Might get your name on a paper or two before you even go to college. So, welcome to Allbright, Prescott."

He nodded and slowly returned to his seat.

"Susan Carver," Ms. Lollyheart called next.

Susan was from Philadelphia. She had founded a literary journal at her school that won first place nationally in her grade level; she was also the teen editor for the *Philadelphia Inquirer*. Her dream was to be the next Maureen Dowd, whoever that was.

Daniel Ellis followed. He was a history buff from Oakland, California, whose specialty was medieval Europe, with particular interest in the Cathars. I was amazed that somebody my age already had a specialty, and I wondered who the Cathars were.

With each progressive student, I was growing increasingly nervous. What was I supposed to say when my turn came? Exactly what special talent should I claim had brought me to Allbright—being Zoë's sister? I wasn't "the best" at anything. I wasn't ranked second, or third, or even two hundred and seventy-ninth in the nation in any subject whatsoever.

"Calpurnia Fiorello," said Ms. Lollyheart. I sat

up straight and peered ahead. Brooklyn did too. How could we have missed her?

When she got up on the dais and turned around, I understood how: She'd lost maybe fifteen pounds, and her face was no longer round. Her eyebrows, noticeably heavy before, had been plucked. And the frizzy ponytail was gone; she'd had her hair straightened and cut in swingy layers. She even had on a little makeup. Cal Fiorello had had a makeover!

"Hi," she said, "I'm Cal. And as you heard from Ms. Lollyheart, that's actually short for 'Calpurnia' . . ."

"Wow, does she look great, or what?" I whispered to Brooklyn.

"I almost didn't recognize her."

The transformation was truly dramatic, but it wasn't just the weight and the hair. The change in her looks had brought about inner changes too. I could see it in the way she carried herself, the tone of her voice, the expression on her face. There was a confidence and a poise that hadn't been there before, and I was glad to see that she no longer looked sad.

". . . who was, by the way, Julius Caesar's wife. You know, the one who told him not to go to the senate on the Ides of March? But do men ever listen to their wives? Of course not!"

She got a big, friendly laugh.

"Anyway, I'm afraid I haven't won any national awards, as many of you have. But since my dad is in the Foreign Service, I've gotten to live all over the world, and that got me interested in languages. I picked up a little Hindi when I was at school in New Delhi and a fair amount of Bahasa in Jakarta. I started learning the Chinese characters when we lived in Hong Kong, but I was pretty young then, so I'm afraid I didn't get very far with speaking it. I was pretty much limited to 'shopping Cantonese.'

"But I've been here at Allbright for three months now—I was in the summer program—and I've had the chance to work with a tutor five days a week . . ."

The summer program—of course! Cal had mentioned it the day we first met. It was one of the reasons her dad wanted her to go to Allbright. Maybe the school was responsible for her new look and personality. I remembered Allison in all her perfection and wondered if there really *was* something about Allbright that brought out the best in people.

"So now I've decided to switch from Cantonese to Mandarin," Cal was saying, "and have been brushing up on my characters and getting a head start on speaking. I'm very excited. The language program here is awesome."

"That's wonderful!" Ms. Lollyheart said. "Here in the U.S., I'm afraid we've fallen rather behind in

43

learning languages. The fact that English is so widely spoken has made us lazy. We desperately need young people like you, Cal. I hope you will try to stretch yourself and take on at least one other language besides Mandarin."

"Actually, I've been giving some thought to Arabic."

"Excellent choice! Thank you, Cal."

As she returned to her seat, Cal spotted Brooklyn and me, and sent us a discreet little wave.

The next kid up was a playwright. He was followed by a political activist and a math genius. Finally it was Brooklyn's turn.

"Knock 'em dead!" I whispered.

"I'm Brooklyn Offloffalof," he said. "And yes, I was born there." The audience laughed, as I knew they would.

"I'm what you might call a hybrid," he went on. "And no, I am not a car."

Everybody giggled.

"I am the product of a Russian Jewish activist poet and an African-American Baptist police officer—and if that's not a hybrid, I don't know what is.

"Now naturally you're wondering how two such people managed to get together. Well, my father was invited to New York to receive an honorary degree from Columbia. Back in those days, in the eighties, Russians weren't free to travel unless they had special permission from the government. And if you were a public figure—a ballet dancer, like Baryshnikov, or a writer, like my dad—they never let you travel alone. They wanted to make sure you didn't defect to the West. I mean, it was pretty grim in Russia back then. Who wouldn't rather stay in Canada or the U.S.?

"So, Dad went to New York, accompanied by a couple of bodyguards, who never left him alone for a second. But the ceremony was in this big hall full of people, and since the commencement speaker was some famous politician, lots of reporters were there, and security too. Dad didn't think his 'handlers' would make a scene in such a public place—terrible press for the Russians—so he decided to make his move. Right in the middle of the ceremony, with everybody watching, Dad got up from his seat, walked over to 'ze most beautifool policeman in the room,' and asked for political asylum.

"So Dad married his 'beautifool policeman' and became an American citizen and moved to Brooklyn, which is where I got my name. He thought it was *so* poetic. My mom could not convince him that a name like Brooklyn was a terrible burden to place on a young child. He promised to let *her* name the next one." Pause. "My sister's name is Junebug."

Hilarious laughter.

"Was she born in June?" came a voice from the crowd.

"Of course."

Brooklyn said all this in a deadpan voice that made it that much funnier. He waited for the laughing to subside, then continued in the same calm manner.

"Last year we moved to Baltimore, where my dad is poet-in-residence in the Hopkins Writing Seminars Program. My mom is with the Baltimore PD."

"And you?" Ms. Lollyheart asked. "Besides having an obvious talent for telling stories, what would you say are your special gifts?"

"Well, first I need to say that my parents come from two of the most demonstrative cultures the world has ever produced, so nothing at our house is ever understated. We actually have exclamation points on our grocery lists: Kleenex! Potatoes! And any little disagreement can turn into this major drama. My dad will bring in the pogroms and the gulags (like they were my mom's fault) and she'll drag in slavery and Jim Crow (like they were his). You feel like you're watching the semifinals of the 'International Suffering Playoffs.'

"Well, in a household like that—and with a name like Brooklyn—I could either spend my life hiding under the bed in terror, or I could pay close attention and use it as material. I'm not really into hiding under beds, so I became a writer instead. My first book of poems is being published by Broadbrook Press in the spring. It's called *In the Shadow of the Bridge*."

No wonder they had recruited him, I thought. Cheez Louise, I was *so* out of my depth! Not that I really had time to brood about this, unfortunately. We had passed Offloffalof and were moving on to Petersen. Either I was going to have to call my mom to come take me home, or I'd better pull myself together and come up with something to say.

At last my name was called. I marched up to the dais with all the dignity I could muster. I had decided there was only one way out of this predicament: I would have to be funny.

"I'm Franny Sharp," I said, "from Baltimore. And I am here to make the rest of you feel brilliant. You probably don't *need* any help with that" (a tittering of laughter), "but I will give it all I've got. I have absolutely no talents, and will endeavor, at all times, to be ordinary. Every bell curve has its two extremes, and I promise to keep a death grip on the bottom end. I am glad to do it. Really, I am. Sydney Carton said it best, in *A Tale of Two Cities,* as he went to his death in another man's place: 'It is a far, far better thing that I do, than I have ever done.' No need to thank me. You're perfectly welcome."

47

I bowed, and the room went wild with cheering and clapping. And then—I swear I am telling you the truth—they gave me a standing ovation!

I returned to my seat feeling wildly elated. My best hope had been to survive the ordeal without making a fool of myself. But I had surpassed that by far. In a room full of geniuses, they'd given *me* the standing ovation! They liked me because I was funny and unpretentious and wasn't a threat to them.

Not the greatest foundation for friendship, you say? I disagree. At least they liked me for who I really am.

5

It was eleven thirty by the time the introductions were over. Ms. Lollyheart congratulated us all on the "hard work and dedication that our incredible accomplishments represented." This kind of startled me for a minute. I had just assumed that success came easily to these kids. They were born smart, end of story. But of course, even brilliant kids have to study. And pretty much all of them had chosen something challenging to do with what little free time they had. They were busy starting literary magazines and founding tutoring programs for inner-city kids while I was home watching old movies on TV. Somehow, this blurred the line between them and me. I might not have their talent, but that was no excuse to float through life.

You'd think this would have depressed me, but it didn't. It made me feel strangely hopeful.

"So that's it for this morning," Ms. Lollyheart said. "Outside, in the hallway, we've set up a desk. If you'll line up there, please, you'll be given your orientation packets. You'll find your schedule for the rest of the week in there, plus a number of forms I'll need you to fill out and return by tomorrow. But most important, the packet contains your cottage assignments.

"I suggest you head directly over to your cottages and start unpacking—the boxes your parents dropped off at the gym this morning should have been delivered to your rooms by now. I want you back here tomorrow at nine, ready to shine. So get a good night's sleep and bring your thinking caps!"

Brooklyn and I made a dash for the door so we could grab a good place in line. About a minute later, Cal joined us. "I'm not cutting in," she assured the girl behind us. "I just wanted to say hi to these two, real quick."

"That's okay," the girl said. "I don't care if you cut." Then turning to the boy behind her, she asked, "Do you?" He said he was cool with it.

"*Really?* That's so nice of you! Thanks!" Cal slipped her arm through mine and gave me a beautiful smile.

"So here we are again, all three of us," Cal said. "Isn't it great?"

We agreed that it was.

"You're going to love it here," she went on. "I promise! Allbright is just the coolest place!"

She reached over and squeezed Brooklyn's hand. "Hey, guy, aren't you going to speak to me?" She flashed a playful smile.

"Can't get a word in edgewise," he said.

"Oh, you!"

I simply couldn't get over the change in Cal. It was like she had switched places with her beautiful, confident, perky twin. I was glad she seemed so happy now, and who wouldn't want to turn glamorous all of a sudden—but I missed the old Cal, that vulnerable, thoughtful, hockey-playing, world-traveling girl I'd met last spring and liked so much. I wondered if her sadness had just been a temporary thing, like a bad mood, and she'd simply gotten over it. Didn't she miss her dad anymore, now that she'd realized what a cool place Allbright was?

"I already know I'm in Larkspur," Cal was saying. "It's the cottage for linguists, so no surprise there. They gave us summer students our assignments ahead of time; they needed us to go ahead and clear our stuff out of Aster—that's where we've been staying—so the new kids could move in. I don't guess there's much chance that either of you will end up at Larkspur, though." She made a cute, disappointed face that reminded me of Allison.

"I'd be willing to bet the ranch on it," I said. "At least as far as I'm concerned. I had this really minimal Spanish program in fourth grade, and every time I'd sit down to memorize vocabulary, I'd fall asleep."

"You'll be in Cyclamen, of course," Cal said to Brooklyn. Cyclamen was full of writers and journalists and playwrights and poets.

"That's what I figured," he said.

"What about you, Franny?" Cal asked. "Got a hunch?"

"Well, not really—since I'm totally without talent and all." They both pooh-poohed this statement, to buck me up, but I kept going. "Not Sunflower; I'm pretty good at science, but I stink at math. And I'm not especially artistic, so it won't be Aster." I was counting them off on my fingers. Including Larkspur, that was three cottages so far that wouldn't want me. It was turning into a rather depressing list of what I wasn't good at. "I'm not really leadership material, so that eliminates Primrose. And—what's left?"

"Geranium," Cal said. "They're policy wonks and economists. Very *not you*. And Violet Cottage. Nobody really knows what Violet is all about, except that the kids there are real oddballs."

"Oh great, that's probably where they'll put me!"

"No," Brooklyn said. "You'll be in Cyclamen, with me."

"I wish. Unfortunately, I'm not a published author."

"You're a reader, though. You're a word person. You quote Dickens."

"True enough."

By then, we had reached the front of the line. No point in speculating any further. Packets safely in hand, we headed out into the sunshine to open them and discover our fates.

"Let's go over there," Brooklyn said, pointing to a circle of benches in the shade of some big, old maple trees.

Cal and Brooklyn opened their packets right away and verified what she already knew and he strongly suspected: Larkspur and Cyclamen. Suddenly I was as nervous as I'd been before the admissions tests. I really didn't want to live in Violet with the oddballs.

"Come on, Franny, open it," Cal said. "We're dying of suspense."

I opened my envelope and pulled out a sheaf of papers in a rainbow of colors. Right on top was my cottage assignment. I held it up to my chest, so they couldn't see it, and smiled.

"What?" they both said together.

Then I turned to Brooklyn and offered my hand for a high five.

"Cyclamen?" he said.

"Cyclamen," I answered.

He got this truly satisfied look on his face and gave my hand a very enthusiastic slap. This was a *lot* of emotion for Brooklyn. He was genuinely happy that we'd been assigned to the same cottage, and I felt strangely proud. This extremely cool person, whom I admired, liked me that much!

"That's awesome!" Cal said, with no apparent sign of feeling left out of this lovefest. She began flipping through her pile of papers. "Want to see if we can sign up for some of the same activities?"

"Sure," I said, my heart still pounding with excitement.

"How about the field trips?" Brooklyn suggested. "Blue sheet."

We all got out our blue sheets and looked them over. There was a trip to the National Gallery, a concert in Shriver Hall, a tour of Ford's Theatre (that's where President Lincoln was shot, in case you didn't know)—and that was just September.

"What's not to like?" Cal said. We signed up for all of them.

"What the heck is this?" Brooklyn asked. He was looking at his orientation schedule. "PD?"

"Oh, you'll love it," Cal said. "That's Personal

Development. You have it once a week, just you and your PD counselor. They videotape you during your first session so you can see how you come across to other people. Then you discuss it and set goals for improvement. Maybe, like, you need to stop slumping. Or you have a tendency to mumble or talk too loud. If you have skin problems, they arrange a visit to a dermatologist. If your hair is really awful, like mine was, they send you to a stylist—"

Brooklyn was staring at her. He looked positively horrified.

"They're gonna give me *grooming* tips?"

"They might," Cal said. "I know you think it's stupid, but you'll be surprised. I found it really helpful. Celebrities and business people pay media consultants big money to get that kind of advice. Don't look at me like that, Brooklyn. You'll love it."

"So is that the deal with your hair?" he said, indicating Cal's new look.

"Yes. And you have to admit I look better."

"I am not walking into *that* trap! No, ma'am! You are every bit as beautiful as you always were."

"Snicker, snicker."

A crowd of sixth graders came flowing out of Willard Theater, all clutching their packets. I searched for the twins and eventually spotted Zoë, surrounded (no surprise) by a cluster of giggling girls. I waved and they headed our way.

"That's my sister."

"Cute," Brooklyn said.

"Yup," I agreed. "Always has been."

Zoë introduced her friends and I introduced mine, feeling rather proud of myself for having two of them already—and here it was only the first day of orientation. The previous year, at the previous school, I'd spent two and a half weeks sitting alone in the lunchroom before I'd finally met Beamer.

"Let me guess," I said. "Primrose." My sister might not know much about foreign affairs, but she had the leadership thing going in spades.

"Yes!" she said, glowing all over. "I guess I'll have to start reading the newspapers, huh? How about you?"

"Brooklyn and I are in Cyclamen," I said, "and Cal is in Larkspur. She's a linguist. She can speak Bahasa and Hindi and is working on Mandarin."

"Wow!" from Zoë and all of her friends. Cal punched my arm in a friendly way.

"Have you seen J. D.?" I asked.

"Yeah," Zoë said, her face clouding a little.

"And?"

"He got Violet Cottage. He says he's okay with it, but I'm kind of worried. I heard this rumor—"

"That it's where they put the oddballs?"

"Something like that. But you know J. D. He said

it'd be more interesting living there. He said he thought the Allbright kids seemed a little too perfect anyway, you know? Remember Allison? And anyway, being weird has always been J. D.'s claim to fame."

"Hmm," I said. "There's some truth to that."

Zoë reached down and squeezed my hand. "We need to go unpack. See you later. It was great meeting you." And they headed toward the cottages. Both Cal and Brooklyn followed her with their eyes. She had that effect on people. Zoë was like a sunset over the ocean; you just couldn't help staring.

"Hey, guys," I said, finally. "Want to look over the PE options? It's the yellow sheet."

"Sure," Cal said, flipping through her papers till she found it. "Anybody into swimming?"

"Yuck!" Brooklyn rolled his eyes. "Swimming laps reminds me of the fifth circle of hell."

"Okay," I said, "are you going to explain that, or do you just plan to sit there and let us feel dumb?"

"Dante's *Inferno*. The wrathful and slothful sinners, sloshing around in the River Styx."

"Thank you," I said. "Such a lovely image. I take it we can eliminate swimming. Tennis, anyone? Racquetball? Hiking?"

"Hiking!" Cal and Brooklyn said together.

"Hiking it is, then." We all checked the little box.

"I think that's it," Cal said. "The rest is just info."

"Time to go unpack those boxes, then," Brooklyn said.

We gathered our papers together, slipped them back into the envelopes, and strolled off in the direction of the cottages. Eventually we reached the turnoff point; Brooklyn and I headed up the hill to Cyclamen, while Cal stayed on the path to Larkspur.

"*Hasta mañana*," I said brightly. "That means 'see you tomorrow' in Spanish."

"No kidding," Cal said.

"Oh, Cal," Brooklyn called. "Don't forget to bring your thinking cap!"

6

"All right," said Ms. Lollyheart. "Will everyone please give me your attention? We need to get started."

The room grew quiet.

"Thank you. I hope you're all settled in nicely at your cottages and ready to give your full attention to our traditional Allbright orientation exercise. I think that by the time it's over, you will have learned a great deal—about yourselves, about this school, about cooperation and leadership, and about the way things work in the real world. It may seem silly at first, but please bear with me.

"Now, to begin, we need to divide you into two teams. Adriana Gomez and Prescott Bottomy, will you please come up to the front?"

My heart sank, because I knew what was coming next. Adriana and Prescott would be asked to choose teams.

Every kid who has ever played baseball knows this routine. It's a chance to shine if you happen to be popular or a really good athlete, but for the poor kid who can't catch a ball to save his life, it's slow death by humiliation. I am not terrible at sports, just not particularly good. As in so many things, I am kind of medium. I can always count on being chosen a little past halfway through. But even once you're safely on a team, it's still gut wrenching to watch those last few kids squirming with shame and embarrassment, wondering which of them will be chosen last.

"Ms. Lollyheart," Prescott said, "can you give us some idea of what our teams will be doing? So we'll know how to choose?"

She gave Prescott a wry smile. "Actually, hon, you won't be needing any kind of strategy today. *I* will be selecting the teams."

I let out a deep breath. Once again, Allbright hadn't let me down.

Ms. Lollyheart proceeded to read out names, and one by one we got up and went over to stand by our team leader. There were twenty of us in total, ten to a team. Brooklyn and I were in Prescott's group, Cal in Adriana's.

Ms. Lollyheart unlocked a closet door and pulled out two large wooden boxes set on little wheels, each with a rope to pull it by.

"Now," she said, "this exercise was designed to use many different talents and thinking styles, all of them abundantly represented here in this room. But what makes it so challenging is that within your teams, you will each work entirely alone on your assigned task—without help from any of your teammates. If each of you does your job properly, then the whole thing should come together like clockwork. Independence and interdependence, just like in the real world."

She raised her eyebrows in an expressive way, and paused for a moment to let what she'd said sink in.

"You will have two days to complete the exercise. At four P.M. on Wednesday, you need to be finished and ready to roll. By then, each team must take the contents of one of these boxes"—she opened a lid and showed us what looked like the sale bin at a hardware store—"and use them to create a robot. It's important to use every item in the box. You will lose points for every piece you leave behind.

"Now, I know some of you hotshots could build a perfectly good robot out of these materials completely on your own, without needing any directions. But chances are that, left to your own devices, you won't figure out how to use all of the pieces and use them correctly. So we have put the instructions

61

on the Internet. Naturally, we didn't want to make this too easy, so don't waste your time looking it up on Google."

"Aw, shucks!" said Claire. She was a National Science Fair runner-up, and you could tell she was cool with any computer challenge you might throw at her. Ms. Lollyheart smiled patiently.

"Now, one of the items in the box is a tape recorder. It's there because your robot is going to tell us the story of its life. One member of your team will be in charge of writing that story. He or she will then pass it on to another member, who will translate it into a special robot language. This language needs to be more or less intelligible to the audience. Be clever—you can do it. And no Pig Latin, please. You're better than that.

"Another team member will read this material into the recorder. So that's five tasks I've mentioned so far: the computer research, building the robot, writing the story, translating it, and recording it.

"Of course, your robot will not just stand still as it talks but will move in expressive and interesting ways. A sixth team member will program it to do these things." She held up an intimidating remote control device with multiple switches and an antenna.

"This is going to be a performance, so the seventh team member will compose the sound track—*original* music, folks, not your favorite rock tune.

And team member number eight will create a back-drop. Number nine is in charge of lighting and any special effects you may devise (You will, of course, be under the supervision of someone on the theater staff. They aren't allowed to help you, but they will make sure you don't destroy the equipment or elec-trocute yourself)."

There was a ripple of nervous laughter.

"And the team leaders?" asked Prescott. "What are we supposed to do?"

"Your job is to run the show. You're sort of like the conductor. You cue the lights and music, and run the robot."

"But, Ms. Lollyheart!" Prescott whined. "What if somebody on the team screws up—like they can't find the instructions on the Internet, or they build the robot wrong? Then that messes it up for the rest of us."

"Exactly," Ms. Lollyheart said, giving him a tight smile.

She paused for a really long time to let this sink in. Then she continued. "Now, the actual presenta-tion will take place over in the arts building, at the Willard Theater. The eighth-grade robot show is at four; we need to be out of there by five so the next group can come in. Okay? Is everybody clear on the assignment?"

"The music and the backdrop," Trey asked,

"what are we supposed to use to make them? I mean, will we have access to musical instruments and art materials and stuff like that?"

"Of course. All that information is in your assignment envelopes—where you are to go and when, what materials are available for your use, everything." She pulled out a fat bunch of envelopes held together with a rubber band. "Now, team members number one need to get on your computers ASAP and try to find those instructions. On Prescott's team, that will be Jenny Kirkland—here, Jenny." She held out an envelope, which Jenny came forward to accept, a stricken expression on her face. She was the political activist who had set up the after-school tutoring program. If she had any special computer skills, she certainly hadn't mentioned them.

"And the computer search for Adriana's team will be done by Daniel Ellis." (In case you forgot, he's the history guy with the Cathars.)

At least he and Jenny would be evenly matched. That's what I was thinking when she called my name—to build the robot!

"But . . . !" Prescott sputtered, beside himself with exasperation (and by now everyone was rolling their eyes and exchanging glances every time he opened his mouth). "Don't I *at least* get to assign my own team members to their various jobs? I mean, no offense, Franny, but I'm sure we could put you to better use doing something—"

"No, Prescott, I'm afraid not," Ms. Lollyheart said. "That's what makes this exercise so interesting: I choose the teams, I make the assignments. Now, for Adriana's team, the robot builder will be Edward Rodriguez."

And so it went. Ms. Lollyheart had rigged this contest so everyone would fail. She had chosen the artists and writers to do the technical jobs and the techies to do the creative stuff. Cal, who could have made up a wonderful robot language, was assigned to lighting. Henry Chow, who had a heavy Chinese accent, was to read the translated story into the tape recorder. And nothing could be more hopeless than asking *me* to build a robot!

It was perfectly clear what they expected us to learn from this exercise—we each have our strengths and our weaknesses, in any society we all depend on one another, yadda, yadda, yadda. I was shocked that they were wasting two whole days spelling out the obvious. And this was an Allbright tradition? Cheez Louise!

"One last thing before you go. You probably *think* you know what this exercise is about, but please, trust me, you are only partially right. It is about many things. It may be years before you really understand it. We have had former students, out working in the business world or in government, who have written us to say that memories of the robot exercise came back to them at the strangest times—and rather often, too. It gave them a window through which they could view the workings of the world.

"All right, you've heard enough from me. You have your assignments. Go forth, my children, and create."

7

I opened my envelope and removed the single sheet of paper inside. It told me to take my box of parts to Room 212 in the science building (advising me to use the elevator, like I wouldn't have figured *that* out for myself) and to wait there until Jenny found the instructions on the Internet and brought them to me. If I chose (or was forced to because Jenny hadn't arrived), I could build the robot on my own.

Once I was finished, I was to take it to Henry Chow in Room 117 of the same building so he could read the robot's life story into the tape recorder (which, by that time, should already have been written by Noah and translated into Robotese by

Martin). Then I was to report to Ms. Lollyheart in the headmistress's office and let her know that I was done. After that I was free to swim, read, nap, or do anything my heart desired until it was time for the robot show.

"Good luck!" it said at the bottom. I was definitely going to need it.

I looked up from the assignment sheet and saw Prescott glaring at me, like it was my fault that I was about to screw things up for the whole team. "What?" I mouthed and shrugged. He turned away.

I rolled my box of hardware over to the science building, thinking gloomy thoughts. While I waited for the unlikely appearance of Jenny Kirkland, I removed all the parts and spread them out on the floor. In addition to about a zillion pieces, some large, some small, they had provided two tools for me to work with: a screwdriver and a pair of pliers.

I began gathering up all the nuts and bolts and separating them into piles according to size. This didn't really accomplish anything, but it was satisfying.

I thought about Beamer and how he liked to take pieces from kits intended for building a bridge or the Eiffel Tower or something and use them to make abstract sculptures instead. I could do something like that with my pile of hardware. It would even be fun. But then of course my team would lose.

Without a robot we wouldn't have a show. I was the weakest link in a long chain of weak links.

Okay, I told myself, *concentrate!* What did this robot need to do? First and foremost, it had to hold the tape recorder. And since it was supposed to be talking, maybe it ought to have a mouth that could move. What else? Well, Ms. Lollyheart had said that it should "move in expressive and interesting ways." Did that mean hand gestures, which meant it needed to have hands? Did it mean dancing, in which case there should be legs? And what about those special effects she mentioned? Was it supposed to blow bubbles? Project slides on a wall? ("This is me when I was just a baby robot!")

I was looking through the parts for anything that reminded me of arms or legs when it struck me that I was totally headed in the wrong direction. I was trying to make a cartoon robot, or something cute out of a movie, like R2D2 from *Star Wars*. But actual, real robots didn't look like people. There was that little vacuum cleaner I'd seen advertised, the one that scoots around your house, bumping into furniture and walls and sucking up your dust bunnies. It's shaped like a hockey puck, but it was still a robot. And what about the machines they use in factories to build cars? Nobody bothers to make them look like little factory workers; they just design machines to do a particular job. If it's supposed to screw two metal plates together, then all they need is an arm with a screwdriver attached to it.

My job, I understood now, was not to be imaginative; it was to be analytical. The key to the design lay there at my feet, in the parts strewn all over the floor.

And so I started arranging them in different ways, noticing things that came in pairs, and things that were one of a kind. I noted where holes had been drilled in the metal—where a bolt was obviously meant to go—and looked for pieces that had the same patterns of holes. There was a reasonable chance they were meant to be bolted together. It was a combination of logic and instinct—like doing a jigsaw puzzle, only in three dimensions.

I was starting to feel (a) a whole lot smarter than I would ever have expected to be in such a situation, and (b) really hungry.

Just then there was a knock on the door, and my heart leaped. But it wasn't Jenny. It was Ms. Lollyheart, delivering a box lunch: a chicken sandwich (with lettuce and tomato, on whole wheat bread), carrot sticks, two small plums, a bottle of springwater, and (naturally) a brownie. I polished them off in no time, then returned to my junk pile.

The tape recorder, I thought, that's the crucial part. So where was it supposed to go? It had a definite shape. Was there anything that looked like it was meant to hold that shape? I crawled around in the mess of metal, searching. And there among the pieces I had set aside as coming in pairs was a half box without a top. Beside it was the other half. The holes lined up. I slipped the two half pieces around the tape player, and they fit perfectly. Plus, the little lip around the edge of the box would hold the recorder snugly in place so it wouldn't fall out, while leaving plenty of room for the lid to open. Great! Now all I needed was to find nuts and bolts of the right size, and put the whole thing together.

I began moving pieces around, trying to come up with a rough plan. I felt amazingly focused, extremely sharp, and forgot for a moment that there was anybody waiting for me, that this was a contest we wanted to win. I wasn't worried about any of that. I was just solving an interesting puzzle.

And little by little, bit by bit, things came to me. Some seemed obvious once I had put them together. The tape recorder, for example, was supposed to go in the back of the robot's box-like head. Others were neat but strange. Like, the robot *did* have a face (though the lips didn't move), and right in the middle of it was an opening that perfectly fit a piece that looked like a nose. Only, for the screw holes to line up, it either had to go in upside down or inside out. What was with that? I shrugged and bolted it on upside down.

The body was made from eight rectangular plates, each about four times longer than it was wide. They overlapped and attached to a small metal ring at the top, then fanned out and were bolted to a larger metal ring at the bottom. The bottom ring had equally spaced attachment points for three little wheels.

I still had a lot of pieces left, and I noticed unused holes near the top of two of the body plates. I decided that's where the arms were supposed to go. There were two pieces that looked like they could be shoulder joints, and they happened to have four screw holes, arranged in a square, matching the plates perfectly.

Unfortunately, I hadn't actually noticed this while I was building the body; I had just put the plates in at random. So now, unless I moved the plates with the holes to their proper location, I'd have one arm coming out of the robot's back and the other out of its side. Not good. I had to unbolt four of the plates and switch them around.

Soon my Tin Man (or "TM," as I now called him) had arms that moved up and down at the shoulder (though they didn't bend at the elbow). Instead of hands, he had little balls with six knobs sticking out of them, like miniature coat pegs. Each ball fit neatly into (and rotated within) a socket, so I assumed they were supposed to spin around.

All that I had to do now was make the thing move—specifically, to make the head nod, the arms go up and down, the hands spin, and the wheels roll. Four moving parts. And happily, my rapidly decreasing pile of parts included four different motors, little black boxes of varying sizes with battery compartments (and yup, they had batteries in them!). Each had a small plastic gear sticking out on one side. There was also a mess of gears and cords and pulleys. I lay down on my back, on the hard floor, and closed my eyes, trying to imagine how they would work.

I had gears on my bicycle. One was attached to the pedals, and it was attached to a chain that turned another gear attached to the wheel. (In the case of the bicycle, I was the motor.) My robot kit had four motors, eight gears, and four chains. How hard could this be?

I had to remove some of the body plates (again!) and part of the head, so I could get inside the robot to bolt in the motors and attach the gears. But everything seemed to fit. And though I couldn't test it (since I didn't have the remote control), I felt sure I had done it right. TM could roll forward and turn, nod his head, flap his arms, and spin his little hands. I had used every part. All that remained were the pliers and the screwdriver. Surely they didn't count.

But just for the heck of it I looked the robot over

for any place where they might go. There was a small hole at the top of his head. I had assumed it was there to let sound out—but now I realized that since the tape player was facing outward, it really didn't need a sound hole. I slid the thin end of the screwdriver into the head, so that only the blue plastic handle stuck out, like a little antenna. It would wobble around when the robot nodded its head, and make a little tick-ticking noise as the metal end tapped against the two motor boxes inside. Maybe that would count as a special effect—altogether *very* nice!

But what about the pliers?

And then it came to me. The nose! That weird upside-down nose was just a holder for the pliers. I slid one handle in and let the rest hang out, and grinned. My robot was as goofy and cute as a day-old puppy.

I packed TM up in his box on wheels and rolled him down the hall toward the elevator, feeling absolutely brilliant, in the zone, clearheaded, and full of joy and energy. The world even looked different—the sunlight coming in through the window at the end of the hall had just the slightest tinge of blue—crystal blue. And everything was sharp and clear, the way distant mountains look out west, where the air is dry.

As I pushed the DOWN button and waited for the

elevator, a sudden surge of pride and well-being washed over me. I had built a robot from scratch. What other surprising things might I be capable of?

I knocked on the door of Room 117 and heard Henry Chow rushing to open it. Judging by the crash, he was in such a hurry that he'd knocked over a chair.

"Henry, meet Tin Man," I said, and lifted my robot out of the box.

"You get instructions?" he asked in his heavy accent.

"No," I said, making a mental note to go find Jenny and tell her she could stop her search. "I built it myself."

His eyes went wide. "Awesome!" he said. "Very awesome!"

"Yes," I agreed, "it is. And Henry—if I can build a robot, you can make him talk."

8

Wednesday night, after the robot show was over, I slipped into one of the common-room phone booths to call Mom and Dad. The booths are very cozy and atmospheric inside, all paneled in wood (except for glass in the folding doors), and there's a cushioned bench for you to sit on. The phones are the old-fashioned kind, with a dial instead of buttons. I had never actually seen one in real life before, only in the movies.

I dropped some coins into the slot and dialed. It made a satisfying *brrrrr* with each spin of the dial, shorter for the low numbers, longer for the high ones. So much nicer than the *beep*, *beep* of push-button phones.

Dad answered, and when he heard my voice, he yelled for Mom to pick up the other line. They were wildly excited that I'd called—you'd think I'd been gone for a year instead of two days.

"How *are* you?" Mom asked, her voice high and squeaky with enthusiasm.

"Great," I said. "I built a robot yesterday!"

"You what?"

"I built a robot. From scratch." And I told them about the assignment and how Jenny hadn't found the instructions on the Internet, so I'd had to figure it out myself.

"Honey, that's amazing!" Dad said.

"And we won the contest. The other robot wasn't built right and it rolled off the stage—*smash*, into the orchestra pit! It was pretty horrible, actually. I felt sorry for the other team."

"It must have been awful," Mom said. "But what an interesting exercise—having everyone work against their strong suits. Clever, actually."

"You know, I didn't think so at first, but now I realize that if they'd assigned me to write the robot's story or something like that, I wouldn't have learned anything new. I mean, I already knew I could do that. But who knew I could build a robot? I still can't get over it."

"Well, we're just as proud as all get-out," Mom said. "And you should be proud of yourself too."

"That's what Ms. Lollyheart said. Actually, she gave a whole speech about it after the show was over."

It was amazing how perfectly I remembered that speech, like I'd had a tape recorder bolted into the back of *my* head too. I swear I could have given it to my parents word for word if I'd wanted to. I didn't though. That would have been a little too weird.

"A whole speech about you?"

"Pretty much. She said I shouldn't put myself down."

"When have you ever done that?" said Dad, laughing.

"When I got to Allbright and was surrounded by geniuses."

"Oh, come on, Franny. You're every bit as smart as—"

"Don't worry, Dad. I was just trying to be funny. And after today my self-esteem is in really, really great shape. Ms. Lollyheart told us that they'd been doing the robot exercise at Allbright since the school was founded, and in all that time, only *two* kids had ever built the robot perfectly. Me and some guy who graduated years ago. Is that cool, or what?"

At the other end of the line I could hear Mom sniffling, like she was blowing her nose. Dad sounded like he was choking back tears, but finally he managed to speak. "Wow!" he said. "Yes, that is cool. You must be walking on air!"

"I'm strangely calm, actually. I just feel really good."

"I wish I could hug you," Mom said.

"I'll hug myself and pretend you did."

"We miss you guys so much," she said then. "Any chance you and the twins could come home this weekend?"

"Gosh, no!" I said. "Saturday is the last day of orientation. And after that, there are all these weekend field trips and lots of activities. And once classes start, there's going to be homework to do. It's going to be hard to get away for a while. But we'll see you at Thanksgiving. That's only a couple of months away."

There was a long silence on the other end of the line. "Zoë is busy too," Mom said glumly. "And J. D. hasn't called once. If you see him, would you please remind him he has parents?" I could tell she was upset. "I have to say, it really bothers me that you don't have phones in your rooms."

"They say phones would distract us from our schoolwork. And they're probably right. I think of all those hours I used to spend talking to Beamer, despite the fact that I saw him at school every day! Maybe that's why I didn't make better grades."

"Franny, that's not the point. We need to be able to reach you when we want to."

"You have the numbers of the phone booths," I reminded Mom. "They're in your parent information booklet. Someone can always run upstairs and get me if I have a call."

"Oh, sure," Mom said, with an edge in her voice. I knew what she was thinking: It would be a real pain for the person who'd have to climb three flights of stairs to knock on my door. Mom wouldn't call me on that pay phone for anything less than the house on fire or Dad in the hospital.

"You couldn't reach us all that easily at camp, either," I said, knowing instantly I had stepped over some line.

"Right," Dad said, kind of snappish. Now he wasn't happy with me either. "Well, I never thought I'd hear myself say this, but I'm buying cell phones for the three of you. This pay-phone business is totally unacceptable."

"Dad, cell phones are strictly forbidden at Allbright."

"Sorry, hon. Sometimes parent rules trump school rules. And this is one of those times."

"But it says, specifically, in the student handbook—"

"Is this Franny I'm talking to? Since when were you such a stickler for rules? Look, they don't want kids taking phone calls in the middle of English class or text-messaging answers to their friends during tests. I can understand that. But they can't object to kids staying in touch with their parents! Just keep your phone in your room, keep it charged, and check it for messages once or twice a day, in case we're trying to reach you. Every now and then you can use it to actually place a call to Dad and me. This is not negotiable, by the way."

The conversation kind of petered out after that. I said that my suite mate was waiting upstairs to teach me how to play chess, so I'd better go.

"We really miss you," Mom said pointedly.

"Don't worry," I answered. "We'll be home in a couple of months."

It wasn't till I was climbing the stairs to my room that I realized what I ought to have said, what Mom fully expected me to say: "I really miss you too."

9

Thanksgiving rolled around and the family was all together again, for four days at least. Aside from the fact that Cal was staying with us for the holiday weekend, everything was back to the usual routine—we were sleeping in our own familiar beds, sitting at our regular places at the dinner table, making the same dumb jokes. You'd think this would all seem perfectly natural to me, that it would make me comfortable and happy. But it didn't. I felt awkward and ill at ease, because now I saw everything through different eyes.

Since I'd been at Allbright, it had become important to me to have everything around me look nice, and be clean, and be in order. Now I saw, for the first time, that 17 Creek Lane was a mess. I don't mean that it was dirty or anything; there was just a lot of stuff strewn around. And things that used to look okay—like the new chenille throw Mom had bought last year to drape over the back of the couch and the decorative pots by the front door that had been filled with red geraniums—didn't look okay anymore. The chenille throw was lying in a pile on the couch where someone had used it the night before. And the flowerpots were still there, only now they held nothing but dirt. How hard could it be, I wondered, to fold up a blanket or haul those pots to the garage for the winter?

Without thinking, I picked up some newspapers from the kitchen table—old papers, I noticed, from the day before—and arranged them in a neat pile on the counter. Dad shot me a curious look, kind of playfully shocked. I smiled and gave a nervous little shrug. I'd need to watch myself, I thought. This was their house, and if they wanted magazines and newspapers strewn all over it, then that was their right. I'd be back in my own room at school by Sunday night.

And anyway, I had bigger things to worry about: Thanksgiving dinner. As I feared, Mom had labored over a meal fit for a plowman (if he happened to be a very important plowman she was determined to impress). In addition to the turkey, there were two kinds of stuffing (one with oysters, one with chest-nuts), mashed potatoes, sweet potatoes, gravy, and white rolls with butter. Basically, it was your tradi-tional holiday meal of meat, bread, bread, bread, potatoes, potatoes, and grease. The only vegetables on the table consisted of beans drenched in butter and sprinkled with bacon bits. Out in the kitchen, I knew, there lurked at least two kinds of gooey pies.

It was one of those impossible situations: I knew from my PD lesson on table manners (and from plain old common sense) that it is unacceptable to refuse food that has been lovingly prepared in your honor, unless it will actually cause you to vomit or will send you into anaphylactic shock. On the other hand, from my nutrition lessons in health class, I knew that virtually every item on the table was sure to clog my arteries, send my blood sugar into over-drive, or simply make me fat.

What to do?

Think before you speak, I told myself. (We were working on impulse control in PD.) *Say something gracious.*

"Gosh, Mom, this is fabulous!" I gushed, and began moving my food around on the plate in such a way that it looked like I'd eaten more than I had. This is a trick they teach you in PD manners class.

"So yummy!" Zoë agreed, doing the exact same thing.

"It's really a treat, Mrs. Sharp," added Cal. "A real home-cooked meal! Thank you so much for going to all this trouble."

J. D. looked up from his plate, studied the three of us for a minute with a baffled expression, did a little eye roll, then went back to chowing down. Clearly he wasn't the least bit concerned about the condition of his arteries.

What? I almost said—and definitely would have said back in the days before I'd learned the importance of curbing my impulses. But I held my tongue, because it's unpleasant to fight with your brother at the dinner table, and especially when you have a guest.

"I don't know what to do about the food situation," I said to Zoë after dinner, while Mom was washing the dishes and Dad was on the couch, sleeping off the four thousand calories he had just ingested. "If this goes on for another two and a half days, they'll have to admit us to the hospital."

Zoë thought about it for a minute, then looked up at me and smiled. "Mom's going overboard because she hasn't seen us in a while. She wants to give us a treat. We need to make her feel okay about cooking healthy food. And I know just how to do it."

Later that night, before we went to bed, we took Mom aside and told her that Cal had recently lost a lot of weight—which was, in fact, the truth—and

85

that she really needed to watch her diet. A master stroke on Zoë's part, I must say! Mom was totally sympathetic and her feelings weren't hurt at all. I predicted that on the following night, we could safely expect broiled skinless chicken breasts and steamed broccoli.

Brooklyn had promised to come by the house on Friday morning—we were such a regular trio that Cal and I missed him already—and I'd invited Beamer to join us too so he could meet my new friends. I'd been looking forward to it all week. Only now, coming home had strangely unsettled me. Suddenly I was terrified that Brooklyn and Cal would find Beamer ordinary—the way they probably thought my parents were loud and my house was messy.

But the thing that worried me the most was that *I* might see Beamer through new eyes too. What if I actually felt embarrassed by him in front of the others? What if I didn't like him anymore? The very thought made my stomach flip. He was the best friend I'd ever had.

Brooklyn arrived first, around ten.

"Omygosh!" I croaked as I opened the door. He'd had a haircut; the dreads were gone.

"Brooklyn, why?" asked Cal. "They looked so cool!"

"Too fussy," he said, passing his hand over what remained of his hair. "Too—defining. I am not, after all, my hair."

"You put it so well," I said. "You must be a writer."

He would never admit it, but I suspected the haircut had had something to do with his PD video. Probably he'd noticed (or his counselor had pointed out) that the dreadlocks were kind of flashy. And the more I thought about it, I realized that they were the first thing you noticed when he walked into a room. With his new look, you couldn't tell right off what sort of person he was. You'd have to talk to him awhile to find out that he was a poet. I had never considered this before—how strange it had been for Brooklyn to go around advertising himself to the world like that. Yeah, the more conservative look had definitely been the way to go.

Beamer was due any minute, and since I already had hair on my mind, I remembered how he tended to go for months and months between haircuts, till he got all shaggy and hippie-like—then he shaved it all off and looked like a Marine recruit for a while. He had, basically, no vanity whatsoever about his appearance. This had never bothered me before. I used to tease him about it because I thought it was funny. Now I realized that he was sending strange messages about himself to everyone he met: This is who I am, a person who doesn't give a flip about how he looks. I wondered if there was some subtle way I could get this across to him without hurting his feelings.

Just then the doorbell rang and Beamer blew in like a storm.

I'm not sure I'd ever seen him that keyed up before. He reminded me of his dogs, the way they would jump up on him and dance in circles and bark hysterically whenever he came home in the afternoons. Beamer didn't bark, of course, but he talked too loud and hugged me within an inch of my life. He greeted Cal and Brooklyn like they were long-lost friends instead of complete strangers. And when Zoë and J. D. came in, he gushed over them, too. He was totally out of control. (My only consolation was that he was in slightly post-Marine-recruit hair mode.)

There was no sitting down for a casual chat. He absolutely *had* to show me the documentary he was working on for his film class. He insisted everybody go immediately into the den, where he hooked up the camera to the TV so he could show us what he had so far. He didn't ask if we actually wanted to watch it. He just assumed we did. I burned with embarrassment.

"Beamer's in a special magnet school for the arts," I explained. "That's why he's taking filmmaking."

"Cool," Brooklyn said.

"Our assignment is to do a documentary on 'what makes us happy,'" Beamer said. "I know that sounds totally sappy, but my teacher says that beginning filmmakers are always doing this dark, depressing stuff because they think it makes them seem profound, when it's actually a lot harder to make a film that's positive and upbeat without being sickly sweet. At the moment I'm still gathering the images. I'll pull it all together and add music at the end, when I do the editing."

"I can tell you really like your new school," I said, hoping I had hit the right note, simultaneously signaling to Cal and Brooklyn that I thought he seemed a little over the top while sounding encouraging to Beamer. It was the sort of subtlety that took a lot of practice to do well, and I wasn't too sure of myself yet. I was afraid maybe I sounded like a total fake.

"Yeah, I do," he said, looking at me curiously, the wind out of his sails a little. "I feel like I belong there."

"That's great," I said lamely.

Beamer's dogs came up on the screen. They were out in the backyard and it was a bright, sunny day, so the shadows from the trees were very dark. The dogs were running in and out of the sunlight, and something about the camera setting made them almost disappear in the glare of the sun, then reappear when they went into the shadows.

"Wow," said J. D., who was now lying on his back (still under the table), watching the TV upside down. "That's so neat!"

Beamer smiled. "Me and my dogs, you know—I couldn't make a film about things that make me happy without them . . ."

I winced to hear him call his video a "film." It sounded so pretentious.

". . . but with dogs, it's hard not to get too cute, you know? That's the challenge. I was trying to find a different way of seeing them."

"I think it's wonderful, Beamer," Zoë said.

"Wait, you'll love this." The scene switched to his living room. The camera must have been set to film automatically, because Beamer was in the picture, sitting on the couch. Again, he'd been thinking about the light, because the window to the west had Venetian blinds and the sun was streaming in, casting a shadow of stripes across him, changing shape with the contour of his body.

Now his largest and oldest dog came into the picture, a white English setter with caramel speckles. He walked stiffly over to Beamer, sat down, and laid his head dreamily in Beamer's lap, closing his eyes contentedly.

"Sweet Sandy," I said.

"Franny's a big Sandy fan," Beamer explained with a happy smile. "Of which he has many. Everybody loves a soft dog."

The camera panned in for a close-up.

"How'd you do that?" Brooklyn asked. "Is somebody else holding the camera?"

"He's got a remote control in his left hand," J. D. said.

"Very observant!" Beamer reversed the picture to show us. "See?" Then he pressed PLAY again, and Sandy made a second entrance.

The scene changed again. Now we were with Beamer's grandfather out in the garage, where he did his "inventing." I guess Beamer was worried that his subjects were all too ordinary (What makes me happy? My dogs! My family!), so he was trying to show them in fresh and original ways. In this case he moved from his grandfather's craggy profile to his working hands, coming in closer and closer till you saw only the fingers.

"I'm thinking, when I have enough footage, that maybe I'll cut each section into bits, and mix them all up. Not just three minutes of dogs, followed by three minutes of Grandpa, and like that. I think I can find natural transition points in each bit that leads to another bit. I'll use music to help me establish a visual rhythm."

At that point Beamer's "film" ended abruptly.

"So, that's it," he said, smiling shyly. "A work in progress."

We all clapped politely, and Beamer looked pleased. I have to say that it was a lot better than I'd expected it to be—though I shouldn't have been surprised. Beamer's very talented.

"Great stuff, man," Brooklyn said.

"Really!" Cal agreed.

Beamer was unhooking the camera from the TV and packing the cables away in his bag. "But I can't do this thing without including Franny."

"What? You don't need me," I said.

"Yes, actually, I do," he said, looking me straight in the eye. "Because you are one of the things that makes me happy."

"Persons. Persons who make you happy. I am not a thing."

"I stand corrected."

He said he wanted me to go up to my room to get my copy of *David Copperfield*. We had done a book report on it together in sixth grade, for extra credit. Actually, I had read the whole thing out loud to him while he worked on his sculpture, since I'm a better reader than he is. It had been the real beginning of our friendship.

"Beamer, nobody wants to watch a movie of me reading a book. How boring is that?" I knew, of course, that I had just been extremely ungracious, and my PD counselor would have been horrified. But I felt confused and self-conscious with everybody watching. This was getting to be too much about Beamer and me, and I was leaving my friends out.

"I think it'd be cool," J. D. said. "I'll get the book. He can pan in on your mouth while you're reading, come in *really close*." He made a funny J. D. face and wagged his tongue around.

I was sure my mouth didn't look like that when I was reading. All the same, I didn't relish a close-up of my lips and tongue moving—and especially my teeth. (My PD counselor had suggested that I might want to consider cosmetic dentistry at some point, and remembering Allison and her dental perfection, I really had to agree.)

"J. D., hold on a minute," I said. "Beamer, I really don't feel all that comfortable with the idea. Can't we do something else?"

Beamer gazed at me for an unnervingly long time. Then he said, "Sure," and put his camera away in the bag.

So we did do something else. We sat around in the living room and talked. I tried to keep the subjects neutral—you know, the weather, books, movies—but somehow the conversation kept straying back to the Allbright Academy: the famous guest lecturer we had just heard the week before, the

Sunday Asian cooking class we had all signed up for, Dr. Gallow's Thursday lectures, our field trip to Ford's Theatre. Then Cal mentioned her mentor.

"You have *mentors* at this school?" Beamer said.

"Oh, yes," Cal said with a lovely smile. "Allbright finds them for us, someone in our field who can help us on our way. Mine's a Georgetown professor of Chinese studies. You won't believe who Zoë's is!"

"Tell me," Beamer said, his voice flat and expressionless.

"Martha Evergood!"

"*The* Martha Evergood? You're kidding me!"

"No," Zoë said. "It's true. And she's an amazing person, too—so funny and kind and down to earth. I mean, here's this lady who has met almost all the world's great leaders and helped shape our country's foreign policy, and she takes the time to mentor kids—five of us from Primrose. She has us over to her house, and next month she's going to take us to a Christmas reception at the British embassy. Can you believe it? We're studying protocol and everything."

Beamer turned to me. "Who's your mentor, Franny?"

"Janice Kline," I said. "She's not famous like Martha Evergood, but she's really neat. A reporter for the *Baltimore Sun*. She took me on a tour of the newsroom last month and she's going to arrange a junior internship for me at the paper this summer."

"You were in Baltimore last month and you didn't call me?"

"Well, it was just a quick visit," I said. "The van brought me in, Janice picked me up at the drop-off point, gave me the tour, took me to dinner, then put me back on the van to go home. I didn't even call Mom and Dad."

"Home?"

"What?"

"You said she 'put you on the van to go home.'"

What was this, anyway? The Inquisition? "I meant *school*," I said, trying not to sound as annoyed as I felt. "Okay?"

"Sure," he said.

I thought Beamer was being unreasonably touchy about the whole thing—I mean, I'd been in Baltimore a total of three hours! I tried to think what my PD counselor would have me do in a situation like this. Change the subject, of course. Talk about something positive.

So I told Beamer about Brooklyn's book of poetry, how it was actually being published and all. Brooklyn rolled his eyes and acted like it was no big deal. "Anyway," he said, "I'm moving in a different direction now. Nonfiction, I think."

"What! You're not going to write poetry any-more?" J. D. asked.

"Sure, I'll always write poetry—for fun. But it's such a limited form. Not enough people read it to make a real impact on society. And that's what we're supposed to be doing, right? Being leaders? Changing our world?"

"Well, yeah," Cal said. "But that's a big switch for you."

"Writing is writing. Anyway, enough about me. It's *your* turn, Cal."

"Oh, no!" she said, but she was grinning.

It was their little joke. Brooklyn was always giving her wacky phrases to translate into Mandarin, like "There's a fly in my wonton" or "Don't strike me with that banana, sir!" Of course, Cal may have just been making stuff up, but it always *sounded* like Chinese.

"In Mandarin, please," Brooklyn said, "Your ice cream is melting on my toupee."

While Cal was thinking, Beamer excused himself, I assumed to use the bathroom. But then I heard him talking on the phone. About twenty minutes later, the doorbell rang. It was his ride home—Beamer's second cousin, Ray, a scraggly-looking kid with acne who was living with Beamer's family for a while, and who played in his dad's rock band.

"You're leaving already?" I said. "I thought you were staying for lunch."

"Yeah," Beamer said, "but I need to go."

96

"I'm sorry," I said. "Is something wrong?"

Ray was still standing there, and it was kind of awkward. Beamer looked unhappy, unsure whether to speak his mind. Finally he took a deep breath. "Something just doesn't feel right," he said.

"I don't know what you mean."

"I'm not sure I do either, but there's something very changed about you. And I don't know how to handle it."

"What do you mean? I haven't changed."

"Yes, you have. You even look different."

"I look better. What's wrong with that?"

"Nothing, I guess. This is stupid."

"I don't know what you want me to do."

"I want you to be yourself. Not some fake, perfect robot person."

"Fake, perfect robot person! Give me a break, Beamer!"

"I'm sorry," he said. "That was mean. Maybe I should leave now."

"He's right, Franny."

I turned around and saw J. D. standing there. "You *have* changed. So has Zoë."

"J. D.! How have I changed?" Zoë asked, truly shocked.

I realized then that everyone had followed us to the door, to say good-bye to Beamer, and that they had been standing there the whole time, listening to us argue. It was a total nightmare.

"Like, you count to five before you answer a question. And you do this squinty thing with your eyes when you smile. And you walk around like you're in a beauty pageant or something . . ."

"Okay, everybody," I said. "Sorry about this. J. D., go crawl back under the table. Beamer, I'll walk you to the car." He said an embarrassed good-bye to Cal and Brooklyn, and we followed Ray down the sidewalk. Ray got into the car while Beamer and I stood there, staring at each other in silence.

"I'm sorry," he said, finally. "I don't know what to say. Maybe next time it should just be you and me. Maybe we can pick up the pieces."

"Sure," I said. And then they drove away.

It would be almost four months before we would talk to each other again.

10

Every weekday afternoon at three we met at the gym for our hike. There were seven different trails on the Allbright grounds, so the PE instructors had divided us up into seven groups and we rotated through the various hikes. Each day they would tell us where our group was supposed to go. We signed in, and then when we got back we signed out again. They wanted to make sure nobody was accidentally left behind on the mountain.

They asked us to keep together for safety's sake, and we tried very hard to do that. But some of us walked much faster than others, and pretty soon we had spread out along the trail. Up front were two very tall senior girls, real power walkers. Judging from their conversation on our first day out, they were in a hurry to get back to their cottages so they could finish up their history papers or Bio II lab sheets or whatever.

Naturally, Cal and Brooklyn and I were anxious to get back to our schoolwork too. But we knew that America's future leaders needed strong bodies *as well* as strong minds. Dr. Gallow had mentioned this several times in his weekly lectures. The PE program was important too. Anyway, we always ended up in the middle, behind the seniors, with three little sixth-grade boys bringing up the rear.

And then, of course, there was Prescott.

I know. What are the odds?

We almost never saw him at school. He wasn't in any of our classes and we lived in different cottages. Even on the hiking trail he walked faster than we did, staying just far enough ahead to be out of sight. This may have had something to do with his natural stride—Prescott does have very long legs. But still. Out of nine people, he was the only one hiking by himself. I actually felt sorry for him.

And while I'm being so fair and reasonable, I guess I ought to admit that the few times we *were* around Prescott he seemed a lot more mellow. Instead of his usual scornful look, he now had this faraway gaze, sort of like he was busy considering all the great matters of the universe. It was a little weird, but a definite improvement. I gave his PD counselor full credit for it.

In early December we had a freak snowfall, ten or twelve inches, turning the campus into a winter wonderland. We assumed we wouldn't be hiking that day; they usually had us run laps or lift weights when the weather was bad. But they had a surprise in store for us.

Snowshoes.

Feeling like arctic explorers, we set out to survey our now familiar woods in winter. For unknown reasons, Prescott decided to join our group that day. Maybe he just couldn't go fast enough on snowshoes to get ahead of us. Whatever the reason, it felt strange to have him along. Cal and Brooklyn and I were such a trio; we had our own little jokes and our way of talking. None of us knew quite what to expect from Prescott.

"I've done this before," he announced. "In Switzerland. You'll get the hang of it pretty quickly. It's not that hard."

Ah, all was now clear. He had joined us to show off his snowshoe skills. And casually mentioning Switzerland—that was *so* Prescott!

I was reminding myself that harmony with my schoolmates was an important life goal, that I was only responsible for my own behavior, not anyone else's, when I stepped on my left snowshoe with my right and pitched over, face-first. I will say this much for Prescott: he helped me up and he didn't laugh.

After a while I did get the hang of it. I forgot about Prescott and just enjoyed walking softly— *pluff, pluff*—on the snowy trail, reveling in the magical quiet of the woods. The branches hung heavy with fat, white dollops of snow, delicately balanced. The slightest breeze or a passing bird was enough to send a fine shower of sparkling white crystals flying into the air.

"It's like some giant sprinkled all the trees with powdered sugar," I said. "Or no, it's thicker than that. How about this: It's like the trees were dipped in tempura batter."

Brooklyn stopped in his tracks.

"Not powdered sugar,
But trees dipped in tempura.
Battered, but not fried,"

he recited.

"What was *that*?" I asked.

"A completely spontaneous haiku." He looked rather proud of himself. "You get eighty percent credit, though. They were your images."

"I thought you didn't write poems anymore," I said.

"Mostly I don't. Poetry isn't an important art form, at least not in terms of influencing the thoughts and opinions of the masses. Hardly anybody reads it. But my counselor said it was all right to play around with poems for fun. Keeps my brain nimble."

"Makes sense, I guess. But you can have credit for the whole thing. It would be nothing without that last line. Not very poetic, though—sorry."

He pretended to pout. "You don't like it? 'Battered, but not fried?' I thought it was witty. Okay. Hold on a minute. How about this:

"Silent, white, and still,
A branch hangs heavy with snow.
Touch it and—beware!"

And at the very moment he said "beware," Brooklyn, who was slightly behind me, delicately nudged a branch with one of his poles and a shower of snow dropped onto my head, enough of it going under my collar and down my back to make me scream.

"Agggh!" I said. "Oh, man, you are *so* asking for it!" I reached down and made a fat snowball, turned around, and smacked him with it. Only then did I notice that Cal was quite a way behind us, standing in the middle of the trail, oddly bent over.

"Cal," I called. "Are you okay?"

"Not really," she said. "My stomach hurts."

"Hurts how?" asked Prescott, who was the first to reach her side.

"A lot," Cal said, and I saw she had tears in her eyes.

"Then we need to turn back," Prescott said, taking charge. "Could be nothing, could be appendicitis. Did it just start?"

"No. It's been coming and going for a while. Only now it's worse. And I . . . feel like I'm going to throw up."

"Come on, let's get you back down the mountain," Brooklyn said.

"I don't think I can walk that far."

"Put your arm around my shoulder."

Brooklyn supported her on one side and I took the other (Prescott was too tall), but it was a total disaster. Cal really didn't have the strength to hold on to us, plus we were walking so close together that our snowshoes got all tangled and we fell in a heap. We stopped for a minute to regroup.

Cal was sitting there in the snow, breathing hard and looking panicked.

I touched her face. "You're burning up," I said.

"I know." And she began to cry.

If we had been characters in a story, we would have gathered branches and made a stretcher or a travois. But since we didn't happen to have any rope or animal hide, we probably would have spent an hour contriving something that would fall apart the minute we tried to use it.

"Let's just carry her," Prescott said.

I had to agree this seemed like the only option. Prescott took Cal's snowshoes off and handed them to me, along with everybody's poles. Then he slipped his arms under Cal's, and Brooklyn took hold of her legs, and they moved along the trail as quickly as they could, trying not to jerk her around any more than necessary. It was awkward and probably uncomfortable, but Cal didn't moan or complain. Then I realized why—she had lost consciousness.

About three minutes later we ran into the sixth graders. They volunteered to run back down and get help. I wondered why I hadn't thought of that myself; it was the obvious thing to do.

Before long, two strapping PE instructors met us on the trail with a stretcher. By the time we reached the bottom, an ambulance was waiting.

We didn't see Cal again for almost two weeks. Her appendix had burst and she was in the intensive care unit of the hospital. Ms. Lollyheart went out of her way to keep us posted on Cal's condition, coming over to Cyclamen to talk to us every day. Cal was still pretty weak from the surgery and the infection, but she was slowly improving and would be good as new in a month or so.

Once she was moved from intensive care to a regular room, she was allowed to have visitors. Ms. Lollyheart took us to see her. To our surprise Prescott was invited to go too. I guess Ms. Lollyheart was under the impression that he was one of Cal's friends.

It was a long way to the hospital, but Ms. Lollyheart knew all the shortcuts. She'd been driving out there every day to see Cal (they let Ms. Lollyheart into the ICU because she was the adult in charge until Mr. Fiorello could get there from Goristovia). I thought it was amazingly sweet of her to go to all that trouble. I mean, between her day job in the headmistress's office and her night job as girls' Mum at Larkspur, she only had a few hours she could really call her own—and she chose to spend them in a hospital with a student. Of course, she was an old friend of Cal's dad and had promised to look after her. That was probably why.

We located Cal's room, but the door was closed; Ms. Lollyheart opened it very quietly. Peeking inside, we were met by a chilling scene: Cal lay woodenly on the bed, both arms straight at her sides, the way I used to put my dolls to sleep when I was little, the covers neatly pulled up to her chest.

An IV tube snaked out of her left hand. Her eyes were closed and her face was thin and ghostly pale. Beside the bed sat a big-chested man with curly, dark hair—Cal's father. He held her right hand in both of his and was leaning over, his forehead almost resting on their clasped hands as though he was crying. In that first horrible moment I thought that Cal had died.

But then the man heard us creep in. He sat up, turned toward us, and whispered, "She's asleep." We were about to tiptoe back out again, when Cal woke up.

"Hey!" she said in a weak voice. "Look who's here! Dad, these are my friends—Franny and Brooklyn and Prescott." She gave us a loopy grin.

"I'm Joe Fiorello," he said, shaking our hands so energetically that it actually hurt. "Evelyn told me what you did, carrying Cal back down the trail, getting help. I can't begin to thank you enough. You may very well have saved her life."

We were at a loss for words. "You're welcome" would have sounded so lame. So we all just stood there smiling sheepishly and not saying anything. Finally I broke the silence.

"All's well that ends well," I said, mentally congratulating myself for finding just the right innocuous comment.

"You must be the poet, right?" Mr. Fiorello

asked. "Quoting Shakespeare?"

"No, Daddy," Cal said, "Franny's the one who built the robot. Brooklyn's the poet. And Prescott's the scientist."

"Actually," I said, "just so you'll know—it's *Brook* now."

"What?" said Cal.

"Pardon?" said Mr. Fiorello.

"His name is Brooklyn, but he prefers to be called Brook."

"Since when?" Cal asked.

"Since lately," he said a little defensively. "Since last week."

"Wow. It's hard to keep track of your identity changes—*Brook*."

"I understand perfectly—*Calpurnia*. At least you were named after Caesar's wife, not one of the five boroughs of New York."

Cal giggled. "Excellent point there. Actually, I kind of like it. Brook. Sounds preppy, like you should have a sister named Muffin."

Mr. Fiorello was trying not to laugh. "You kids go ahead and have your visit," he said, making room for us by the bed. He went over and joined Ms. Lollyheart, who had been waiting near the door.

"Anybody else changed their name since I got sick? I hate to be out of the loop, guys."

"All right, Cal," Brook said, changing the subject,

"let's see how well you're recovering. Can you say, 'Nurse, there's a slug in my bedpan'—"

"Sorry, no," she said. "My brain's not up to Mandarin translation yet."

"Just trying to cheer you up."

"Don't worry. I'm plenty cheery," she said. "My dad's here." She gazed adoringly at the far end of the room, where Mr. Fiorello was chatting quietly with Ms. Lollyheart.

"Yeah," I said. "At least *something* good came out of being sick." *For a while at least*, I thought. It was the perfect setup for heartbreak. Here was Cal as happy as a clam, Daddy by her side. Then the next thing she knows he's getting on a plane for Goristovia. It wasn't going to be easy.

Just then Prescott, who had been really quiet on the drive out to the hospital and had not spoken since we entered the room, finally opened his mouth.

"Cal," he said, "I need to ask you something. You had to have been in a lot of pain when we left the gym. What on earth possessed you to go up the mountain in that condition?"

I was shocked. "Cheez, Prescott," I said. "Leave her be!"

"No, actually that's a good question," Cal said. "I've been asking myself the exact same thing. There are some easy answers I could give, like I thought the pain would go away, or I didn't want to ruin everybody's good time, which is pretty ironic—since I ended up ruining it big-time, didn't I?"

"That doesn't matter," Brook said. "It's not important."

"Yes, actually, it is," Prescott said. "Because what she did was reckless."

"You know, Prescott, sometimes—"

"Hey!" Mr. Fiorello said. "Let's everybody cool down, please. This is a sickroom."

"Sorry." Brook was staring daggers at Prescott.

"Guys," Cal said. "Prescott has a point. What I did *was* reckless—which strikes me as weird, because I'm not usually a risk taker. There was something very complicated and interesting and psychological going on. I'll get back to you when I figure it out. Okay, Prescott?"

"Yeah," he said. "Do that. Because, you know what, Cal? You might have died. And believe it or not, I care what happens to you."

Two and a half weeks after she went into the hospital, Cal came back to Allbright—but not to Larkspur Cottage. She had to spend several more weeks recovering in the infirmary. That carried her right through Christmas and into the New Year, which meant we didn't get to spend the holidays together, as we had planned. I was really sorry about that, though it wasn't entirely bad. For one thing, with the week-and-a-half-long winter break, Cal wouldn't be missing quite so many classes as she would have if she'd gotten sick in, say, February. And since I didn't have Cal as my houseguest, I was able to use the free time to get ahead on my schoolwork and do some advance studying for midterms.

Mr. Fiorello hadn't been around for Christmas either. As soon as Cal was out of the hospital, he'd flown back to Goristovia—and her happiness went with him. Now Cal was a total mess, like she'd been when I first met her.

I discovered this when school started up again and Brook and I went over to the infirmary to see her. It turned out to be a very unpleasant visit. I wasn't used to being around that much negative emotion. Allbright kids are a cheerful bunch, and you kind of get used to it. Everybody's pleasant all the time. It's really nice. So to suddenly be with someone who's absolutely miserable and who inflicts their pain on you—well, it's really uncomfortable. As Dr. Gallow has pointed out in his lectures, everybody has problems in life, but what's the point of dwelling on them? And really—isn't it just good manners to keep your misery to yourself?

Much as I loved Cal, I really felt she needed to pull herself together and stop moping. Develop a more positive outlook on life, so that people wouldn't hate being in the same room with her.

Of course, I didn't say any of this to her. She *was* still recovering from a terrible illness, and I figured I ought to cut her some slack. Unfortunately, I couldn't think of anything *else* to say, and since Brook was unusually quiet and Cal was depressed and withdrawn, we were stuck with this really awkward silence. It was awful. *Somebody* had to say *something*.

Finally, spotting a pile of books on the table, I said, "Oh! So you're starting to get caught up on your schoolwork. That's great!"

"Yeah," Cal said. "I have a tutor who comes by in the mornings and works with me. Mr. Canaday. He's really nice."

"Great! I should have known that Allbright would do something like that, give you a private tutor. Isn't this an amazing school? We're so incredibly lucky—"

"Yeah, but to be honest, I'm kind of not in the mood for schoolwork right now."

"*Really?*" I was shocked. "Why not?" She had missed so much school, she was so far behind. If it had been me, I would have been frantic by this point. "Don't you want to get caught up? You have all this time, sitting around in the infirmary. You shouldn't waste it doing nothing."

"I'm doing something. I'm thinking."

"Never too late to try something new," Brook said, managing to be funny and at the same time move the conversation away from gloom and doom. He's better at that sort of thing than I am.

"True," Cal said, not cracking a smile. She seemed to be studying an empty spot on the wall behind us.

I couldn't stand it any longer. It was the old "elephant in the room" thing. Maybe it would be best just to get it out there and deal with it. I reached over and touched her arm. "Cal," I said, "we know how much you miss your dad. We're really sorry."

She nodded slowly but didn't say anything. I heard Brook, behind me, give a quiet little sigh. There really wasn't anything left to say.

"We'll be back tomorrow," I said.

"Sure. Thanks for coming."

Then, just as I was about to shut the door, Cal called me back. "Franny," she said, "will you do me a favor?"

"Sure. Anything."

"Ask your brother a question for me."

"All right." That seemed weird. "What?"

"Do they serve brownies in the Violet Cottage dining hall? Will you ask him that for me?"

11

By the end of January the weather was warm again. The snow had long since turned to slush, then disappeared. And Cal, who was finally declared fit to return to normal life, was back on the trail with us.

Since that day in the snow Prescott had made himself a regular part of our hiking group, and we actually didn't mind all that much. His social skills had continued to improve—he even made jokes sometimes. Not often, but now and then. We *almost* kind of liked him.

Now, the particular day I'm about to describe to you—a very important day, a turning point in this whole story—started out no differently from any

other, except that Cal seemed quieter and more thoughtful than usual. (She'd stopped being moody and depressed, thank goodness, but she'd never bounced back to her perky old self.)

We'd been hiking for about twenty minutes when she stopped and pointed to a cluster of fallen logs just off the trail. "Mind if we sit down over there for a minute?" she asked. We figured she was tired and needed to rest. We said that was fine, and everybody found a place to sit.

"There's something I need to tell you guys," Cal said. "It's really important. I just hope you're not going to think I'm crazy."

Brook raised his eyebrows. "Wow! Can't wait to hear *this*!"

"You've got to listen to the whole thing, though, before you decide to haul me off to the loony bin. Okay? It's complicated."

We agreed, though at that point we still thought it was going to be funny.

"You know I wasn't able to eat anything for a long time after the surgery," she began. "They fed me through an IV tube. Then once the infection was under control, they wanted me to start eating again. They wouldn't let me leave the hospital till they knew my, you know, *plumbing* was back in action."

"Uh-huh," Brook said. Where *was* she going with this?

"As soon as I got past the broth and Jell-O stage, Ms. Lollyheart brought me a basket of brownies."

"Yeah, always with the brownies," I said.

"Exactly. I was polite and thanked her, of course, but they were the last thing in the world I wanted to eat. So, I threw them away."

"Okay," Prescott said slowly. He was watching her like a hawk, probably wondering why Cal thought her digestion and eating habits were a subject of special interest.

"Well, so then I moved over to the infirmary, and they brought in my food from the main kitchen. The usual yummy stuff, only I still wasn't hungry. I tried to eat, but nothing tasted good to me, so I mostly picked at my food. The nurse kept nagging me to eat more and—here's the strange part—when I told her I absolutely couldn't, she said, 'Well, *at least* try to eat your brownie.' I thought that was weird. Don't you?"

"Not really," I said. "They're full of vitamins and fiber and stuff, remember? They're good for us."

Cal shook her head. "Come on, Franny, think about it. We're already taking vitamins. And the food here is incredibly nutritious. So what's with the brownies?"

I shrugged.

"Well, hold that thought. We'll return to it. So,

anyway, after a while I got so sick of the nurse bugging me to eat the brownies that I started crumbling them into the potting soil of that poinsettia you guys sent me. When she'd come back to get my tray, she'd be *so* psyched that I had eaten my brownie like a good girl. Never mind that I hadn't touched my fish and had only eaten three green beans and, like, a bite of salad.

"Do you remember, back then, that I said I'd been doing a lot of thinking? Well, here's what I was thinking: I noticed, shortly after I got here last summer, that I couldn't *feel* anything anymore. I'd think about my dad, and how I'd hardly ever see him and how he was in so much danger, working where he does. And nothing came. No emotions. Nothing at all.

"I talked to my PD counselor about it, and she said I was just making a wonderful adjustment to a situation that was beyond my control. It was a healthy response. And I thought that made sense. I was glad about it. I had spent too much of my life feeling miserable, you know?

"When my mom found out she had cancer, it was already too late. It had spread and she didn't have much time left. So she made me this video. Every time she thought of something she wanted to tell me, that she thought I'd need to hear some time in

117

the future, she would set up the camera, sit in front of it, and talk. She must have worked on it for weeks, because she had on, like, twenty different outfits over the course of that video. I think it's what kept her going, there toward the end, the thought of giving me motherly advice from the grave. For a long time after she died, I would watch that thing compulsively, over and over, crying and just wallowing in grief.

"Then when I finally got over *that*, and was moving forward and cheering up a little, my dad started drifting out of my life, and it began all over again, the grief and the self-pity. Between one thing and another, I've been a total basket case for a good part of my life. So naturally, when I got to Allbright and stopped feeling all that pain, it was, like, this huge relief. I thought, boy I must have been really depressing to be around! How could anybody stand me? And by the way, Prescott, while I'm on the subject, I have an answer to your question now—about why I went up the mountain when my insides hurt: because I couldn't bear to be Cal-who-is-forever-having-problems anymore. I was determined to be cheerful no matter what. I would just tough it out and smile through the pain."

"Pretty good analysis, Dr. Freud," Prescott said. "But what you did was still incredibly stupid."

"Gee, thanks," Cal said.

"You're welcome."

"Cal, we're still waiting to hear what this is all about," I said.

"I know. Sorry. So, anyway, I had this feeling I was really a changed person, like I said. Did any of you notice that I was different?"

"Yes," Brook and I said in unison.

"Okay. There were other things too. Schoolwork was easier for me than it's ever been before. I felt smarter all of a sudden, and more motivated. Things didn't distract me so easily; I could concentrate and remember things incredibly well. All of this was totally awesome! But I did have these weird visual sensations, especially the light. It seemed brighter and clearer and—"

"—blue," Prescott said.

Jaws dropped all around. "Yes," I said. "Me too. It wasn't dramatic or anything, but I noticed."

"Aha!" she said. "This is going to be easier than I thought. Didn't any of you think that was strange?"

"I did at first," I admitted. "But it was so subtle— and pretty soon I got used to it. It started to seem normal."

"I actually mentioned it to my PD counselor," Brook said. "She told me it was just the quality of the light in the mountains. Said everybody comments on it when they get here."

We were all quiet for a while. Then Prescott cleared his throat. "Come on, Cal, you're going in about ten different directions here. Where are you headed with all this?"

She sighed. "Okay. Franny, do you remember when Brook and I were at your house and your friend came over?"

"Beamer."

"Yeah, Beamer. And he was leaving and you were having a fight, only we accidentally overheard?"

"Yes." Not a moment I cared to recall.

"Do you remember how Beamer said you had changed? And J. D. jumped in and agreed—said that Zoë had changed too?"

I nodded.

"Well, when I was lying there in the hospital and later in the infirmary, I started putting all this stuff together. Why do kids change so drastically when they come to Allbright? Why are the students all so perfect? No bullies, no dummies. Everybody is good-looking and well-behaved and polite and cheerful and tidy and ambitious. Does that sound like any normal group of kids you've ever known before?"

"We're a picked group," I said. "So we've already got a head start. Then they teach us to maximize our potential, help us discover our weak spots so we can work on them. It's not mysterious. Why shouldn't we be successful? And frankly, I'm glad there aren't any bullies here and everybody is nice."

"Yeah, I know all that, and I don't care much for bullies either. But I want you to ask yourself this: Why are we all so *compliant*? Even Brook—remember how you made fun of PD when you first got here? 'They're gonna give me *grooming* tips?' Two months later, your counselor says your dreadlocks look 'fussy' and you go and cut them off. And then suddenly you're dropping poetry in favor of something that 'increases your impact on society.' And you change your name to something more conventional. I'm not picking on you, Brook. We've all changed. Whatever they tell us to do, we do. Only, apparently, that's not the case with J. D. You have to wonder why.

"Of course, I didn't know your brother before, Franny, but he doesn't seem like your typical Allbright student to me. He's not all . . . *polished,* you know? He doesn't have that 'little adult walking around in a child's body' sort of feeling about him. He's just a regular ten-year-old kid."

"Eleven."

"Fine, eleven. But my point is, he's normal. Tell me honestly, has J. D. changed since September?"

"Not really."

"Aha. So maybe that's why he could see what was happening to *us*."

"But—," I said.

"Let me finish, please. Then you can ask questions."

"Okay."

"So I started thinking about how the kids over at Violet Cottage are called the Allbright oddballs. But they aren't really all that odd. They're no different from lots of kids at my other schools. They just *seem* odd by comparison to the rest of us because they haven't had the Allbright makeover. So I started to wonder if there was something different going on over at Violet Cottage, something that would explain why *we* had changed and J. D. hadn't. Franny, remember the question I asked you, when I was in the infirmary?"

"Yes."

"Well, did you ask him? Did you ask J. D.?"

I nodded. "He said they do *not* serve brownies over at Violet cottage."

Cal smiled in satisfaction. "Everybody following my drift?"

Nobody said a word. The tension was so thick you could swim through it.

"C'mon, people! J. D. wasn't being medicated, so

he noticed the difference! He could see how the rest of us have changed."

"*Medicated?*" This from all three of us, in unison.

"The brownies," Cal said. "They've been medicating us with the brownies!"

Brook literally recoiled at the suggestion. "Oh, please!" he said. "That's ridiculous, Cal. Why on earth would they do that?"

"To create designer children, I guess. Perfect products. So much easier to teach."

"How could you possibly believe that?" I said. "They have our—"

"—'best interests at heart.' That's what you were going to say, right?"

"Something like that."

"And then one of you" (she pointed first to Brook and then to Prescott) "was going to say, 'We're all so incredibly lucky to have the opportunity to maximize our potential so we can be of service to this great country of ours.' Tell me honestly that you weren't."

Nobody said a word. It was a horrifying moment.

"We've been programmed, guys," she said. "Those lectures Dr. Gallow gives us every week, we never question any of it. We accept it like God's gospel truth. I did the same thing, but then I stopped eating the brownies and came to my senses."

Prescott shook his head. "You're wrong," he said, "shockingly wrong."

"All right, Prescott," Cal countered. "You're a scientist. You believe in the scientific method, right?"

"Yes."

"Then let's try an experiment. Let's *prove* this thing one way or another. Am I shockingly wrong—or am I shockingly right? For one month, all three of you stop eating the brownies. During that time, I won't say another word about it. But on February twenty-seventh, one month from today, let's talk again. Are you willing to do that? In the interest of science—and the truth?"

"They expect us to take the brownies in the dining hall," Brook said. "It'll seem weird if we don't."

"No problem. Just take one when you go through the line, then when nobody's looking, wrap it up in a napkin and stick it in your pocket. Throw it away later."

Brook nodded. "Okay," he said. "That works."

And so we agreed to try the experiment, though I think I can speak for the others when I say we all felt terrible about it. We loved Cal, but we also felt incredible allegiance to the school. Sneaking around, disposing of napkin-wrapped brownies, just considering the *possibility* that they might be doing something bad to us—it all felt so sleazy and disloyal. Because, you see, I really *did* believe that the Allbright Academy had my best interests at heart. I really *did* feel incredibly lucky to have the chance to maximize my potential. . . .

12

February 27 arrived and we had our meeting. But it was only a formality. We had already been feeling (and discussing) the changes for a week by then. Like Superman gradually losing his powers—the flying and the X-ray vision and all that—we were turning back into plain old Clark Kents. It was disturbing for all of us, each in our own unique ways.

Cal, of course, was ahead of the rest of us, but she continued to struggle with her emotional life, without the joy juice or whatever it was they had put in the brownies. She was learning how to be happy on her own, to come to terms with her personal tragedy. Apparently, she found this a life-changing and empowering experience. It was like she'd gained a new and permanent type of superpower: the ability to deal with her own feelings.

Not surprisingly, Prescott didn't say much about what *he* was feeling, but I suspect it was a little humbling for him to discover that his famous brilliance had not been entirely his own—that now, without chemical assistance, it had slipped a notch. He was still a great student, as he'd always been, but not as great as he had come to think he was. Since being the best at everything was Prescott's reason to live, this was no small deal.

Brook, to the dismay of his PD counselor, changed his name back to Brooklyn, started growing out his hair, and went back to writing poetry. He was incredibly angry about the whole brownie business, which kind of surprised us—he had always been so mellow. But once he saw how much of his individuality he had given up so he could play out some life scenario the school had written for him, he was devastated. He couldn't believe he'd been so compliant. He was so full of shame and rage that, for a while there, I really worried about him. But he poured a lot of it into his poetry, and that seemed to help. He finally got back the old Brooklyn calm that had helped him through his weird family life all those years.

As for me, I learned to accept being ordinary

again. Studying wasn't such a breeze anymore, I was no longer compulsively neat, and I couldn't always concentrate on my schoolwork. Sometimes I didn't even *want* to concentrate on my schoolwork. And then, of course, there were the emotions: I actually felt them, the highs as well as the lows. But none of this bothered me nearly as much as the memory of how horrible I had been to Beamer and my family. What a totally creepy, prissy, awful person I had been! It kept me up at night, just thinking about it.

And while I'm on the subject of my family, that was something else I was struggling with at the time—whether or not to tell Mom and Dad about Allbright and the brownies.

I had, after all, two perfectly normal, loving parents who wanted to be involved in my life—unlike Cal, whose dad was far away (both emotionally and physically), or Prescott, whose parents didn't seem to give him much thought, or Brooklyn, whose mom and dad were too intense to deal with. I had none of these problems, and I really felt my parents deserved to know what was happening to me.

And yet. And yet. If I *did* make that phone call, the repercussions would be huge. Not only would Mom and Dad yank us out of Allbright in a heartbeat, they'd make a huge stink—complain to the school, call the papers, call the police. What sane parent *wouldn't* do those things? And then the bad guys—

whoever they were—would have plenty of warning to cover their tracks or flee to Brazil. I didn't plan to hang around Allbright forever, but now that we had an inkling of what was going on at the school, I wanted to see the thing through.

And so, even though it made me feel squirrelly inside, I decided not to tell my parents—at least not yet. I made up for it by taking Zoë aside and telling her to stop eating the brownies (no need to tell J. D.—he wasn't eating them anyway). I said she had to do this secretly, that I'd explain everything to her later, when I knew more, but she'd have to trust me for the moment. That bought me some time. Now all we had to do was get some solid proof against those scumbags so we could nail them to the wall. (Yeah, okay, I watch too many old movies.)

It was Brooklyn who came up with a plan to get us started. He pointed out that it would be a really good idea to get our hands on some of that brownie mix so we could see what was in it. So the next day after classes were over, he skipped PE (claiming he had twisted his ankle and wanted to stay off of it for a few days) and went over to the central kitchen. (All the school's food is prepared in one place and then delivered to the various cottages.) He just walked in the door and went up to the first person he came to, a guy who was busy chopping onions. Brooklyn explained that he had gotten into trouble, and as punishment he'd been given the choice between a week of detention and a week of work duty. He'd chosen the work, so they had sent him over to the kitchen to make himself useful. Help sweep up and stuff.

"That's Reuben over there," the man said. "He's the guy you need to talk to."

Brooklyn repeated the same story to Reuben, who looked surprised.

"I never heard of work duty at Allbright," the man said. "Or detention, either. What the heck did you do?"

"Well, um, I burned a letter. And unfortunately, there's not actually a fireplace in my room."

Reuben heaved a big sigh and looked disgusted. "You set your *room* on fire?"

"No. Just, you know, set off the smoke alarm. Anyway, here I am, at your service."

Reuben grunted and looked around to see what needed doing. "Well, you can rinse out those trash cans. Empty 'em in the Dumpster, then take some of that detergent there, and the hose out back, and clean 'em out."

So that's what Brooklyn did, all afternoon. The next day, he was back.

"How long you in for, anyway?" Reuben asked.

"A week."

"Hmm. Well, okay, see those canisters there? Marked 'sugar,' and 'flour,' and stuff? You can top 'em off. Take 'em into the storeroom—c'mon, let me show you."

Brooklyn tried hard not to grin. Like Brer Rabbit and the briar patch, the storeroom was the very place he wanted to be! He ever so casually picked up his backpack and carried it in there with him.

"Set your canister on the table, here. See? Now, since this one says 'flour,' you go over to the shelf here, where the big bags of flour are, and you take the clip off and *very carefully* pour it in. Don't be making a mess, now, okay?"

"I won't."

"Wipe the canister down with a damp cloth before you put it back on the shelf in the kitchen. There's always a little flour dust gets on the outside, and then it gets on the shelf. We like to keep a clean kitchen."

Finally Reuben couldn't think of any more instructions for what was, basically, a really easy job. He went back to his own work and left Brooklyn to it.

As soon as he was alone in there, Brooklyn started searching for anything that looked like brownies or brownie mix. It was a big storeroom and there was a lot of stuff in there. After about five minutes he figured he'd better finish with the flour canister and move on to another one. He didn't want to arouse suspicion.

After the flour, he filled the sugar canister and searched the shelves for another few minutes. He did the same with the salt, the rolled oats, and so on.

Then he lifted the next canister down from the shelf. Brownie Mix, it said.

Finally!

After ten minutes of fruitless searching, he went to find Reuben. "The brownie mix," Brooklyn asked. "Where is it?"

"Oh, yeah. I'll show you." He slid a cardboard box off the bottom shelf. "I don't know why they can't pack this stuff in smaller boxes," he grumbled. "Weighs a ton." He lifted out a large Ziploc bag full to the brim with brown powder. There was a label stuck on the bag; it looked like somebody had made it on a computer. Brownie Mix, Recipe Variant II, it said. Then there were instructions—how many eggs to add, how much oil and water, what temperature to cook it at, and so on.

"Keep the mix in the bags," Reuben said. "It's already pre-measured. Makes it easier for the cooks. Just slide the bags into the canister like this."

"What does that mean, Recipe Variant II?" Brooklyn asked.

"Oh, that's the regular mix. They just use Recipe Variant I at the start of school and after long vacations. Then they got Recipe Variant III—that's for the baskets they send home for Thanksgiving and Christmas and spring break. Beats me why. They all look exactly the same. Maybe they're different flavors or something. Anyway, you got the drill?"

Brooklyn said yes and picked up a handful of fat Ziploc bags. The minute Reuben left, Brooklyn slipped one into his backpack.

So, now that we had a sample of the brownie mix, Prescott said he could take it to his mom's lab over the weekend and run a chemical analysis on it. While he was at it, he decided to check out our multivitamins, too. His cover story, as far as his parents were concerned, would be that he was finishing up a chemistry lab assignment.

"But you're not taking chemistry," I said.

"Yeah, but Mom doesn't know that."

"She doesn't know what *classes* you're taking?" I was astonished. My parents knew the name of every teacher I had (before I went off to Allbright, anyway), when I had a math test, what book we were reading in English, what sport we were doing in PE—the whole nine yards.

"My parents don't really get into the details of my life," Prescott said. "As long as I make straight A's and take the most advanced classes and get medals on awards day, they're happy."

"Won't they notice, when your report card arrives and it says 'biology'?"

"Nope. 'Fraid not. They'll just check to make sure I got all A's."

I felt truly sorry for Prescott just then. From the sound of it, he was little more than a life accessory to his parents—like the right house or the status car or the degree from the best university. Prescott excelled at the things they valued most. He rounded out their successful lives. "Our son? Oh, yes, he took the science, computer, *and* Latin prizes at school—but then he always does." A few years down the road they'd be mentioning that he was at Harvard or Yale. And later still that he was at work on his doctorate from MIT. But as for the actual living Prescott, they didn't pay much attention to him.

That said, at this particular moment it was actually very convenient that he had such clued-out parents. He could just walk into his mom's lab at Johns Hopkins and use the equipment and the chemicals and get help from the lab assistants. And no one would bother asking questions.

Now, while Prescott was trying to figure out what had been added to the brownie mix, Cal and I had our own job to do. We spent the weekend at my house, preparing look-alike bags of ordinary commercial mix for Brooklyn to take over to the kitchen and substitute for the Recipe Variant II. Unfortunately, this meant making up a cover story to tell *my* mom too, which made me feel even squirrellier than I already did. I just kept reminding myself that I was trying to save a lot of kids from eating Recipe Variant II—and with any luck, nail those scumbags.

What I told Mom was that Allbright was involved in a community-service project—taking brownie mix to homeless shelters and soup kitchens. This story was *slightly* less ludicrous than it sounds, because Mom knew all about the famous healthy Allbright brownies (the school sent a basket of them home with each of their students at Thanksgiving and Christmas breaks—and of course we now knew *why*). So, bringing such a nutritious and tasty treat to homeless people sounded fairly reasonable to her. Only she didn't understand why we were buying commercial brownie mix instead of giving them the special healthy kind. Also, why did we have to empty all the mix out of the boxes it came in and transfer it into Ziploc bags? These were very good questions.

"Well, see, the brownies we have at school don't have any sugar in them. That's good for us, since we have plenty of nutritious food to eat. But these people don't have a steady diet, and they can really use the calories. So what we're supposed to do is take the commercial mix out of the boxes and put them in the Ziploc bags. Then we deliver them to the kitchen at school, where they unzip the bags and add the wheat germ and vitamin powder and fiber and stuff to the mix. The school *could* have done it all themselves, but they wanted to get the students personally involved. To set an example of public service."

It's embarrassing what a good liar I am. I prefer to think it's due to my lively imagination rather than any criminal tendencies. But the bottom line is, my story worked. Mom not only didn't question us further, she agreed to take us shopping and pay for the mix and the bags and the stick-on labels. And she didn't mind that we took over the kitchen to pour all that mix into all those Ziploc bags (though she did make sure we cleaned up afterward).

Cal and I had brought our backpacks home empty. Now we filled them to bursting with bags of fake Recipe Variant II. There were still quite a few bags left over, so I dug around in J. D.'s closet and found his old Chipper Chipmunk backpack from second grade and filled it up too. When we carried them back to Allbright, who was to know they weren't full of books?

We met on the trail the following Monday to report on our various activities. Prescott said it was going to

136

take him a little longer than expected to finish the analysis, but he *had* found out a few things, which were as follows: (a) the vitamins were just vitamins, (b) three different chemical compounds had been added to the brownie mix, and (c) it looked like all three compounds were previously unknown. He thought this last part was particularly interesting. I thought it was particularly creepy. The scientist who had been helping him had agreed to keep working on the chemical analysis for him during the week, which would definitely speed things up.

The delay wasn't really a problem, though. Whatever those compounds were, they didn't belong in the school's brownies. So the first order of business was to get the bags of Recipe Variant II out of the boxes in the kitchen storeroom and replace them with bags of plain old ChokoDream—which is why Brooklyn wasn't there for our meeting on the hiking trail. He was back in the kitchen with his new friend Reuben.

The night before, Brooklyn and I had done one of those cool trade-offs, like they do in the movies, where two guys sit next to each other on a train, each carrying an identical briefcase. They put them on the floor at their feet, then when it comes time to leave, they make the switch by casually picking up each other's briefcase. Only we did it in the dining hall, with backpacks. (Yeah, I know, we didn't really need to be that subtle. But it felt so cool.)

When I got back to my room, I locked the door, took all the bags of brownie mix out of J. D.'s Chipper Chipmunk backpack, transferred them to Brooklyn's empty backpack, and set it aside. The next night we'd do the trade-off again. Later, he and Cal would meet at the circle of benches to do the third switch. Brooklyn would have all the bags of regular brownie mix safely in his room. The rest was up to him.

"Not again!" Reuben said. "What now?"

"It involved a water balloon. Not so bad, really— but it was a second offense."

"You are something else, dude."

"You miss me?"

"Didn't have time to."

Brooklyn didn't get anywhere near the storeroom that Monday, but he did accomplish something important. Reuben set him to wiping down all the counters with Clorox. When Brooklyn reached the part of the kitchen where all the canisters were, it occurred to him for the first time that the cooks would use the brownie mix in the canisters first— and only *then* would they go to the box in the storeroom. If we wanted to get this thing started right away, the canisters were the place to begin.

And so, when Reuben was safely occupied elsewhere (and everybody else seemed too busy to care), Brooklyn took all the storage canisters down and began wiping the shelf with Clorox too. Once he had all those canisters spread out on the counter, no one would notice that one of them went missing for a few minutes—because Brooklyn had carried it off to the broom closet, where, in almost complete darkness, he took the nine remaining bags of Recipe Variant II out and put bags of ChokoDream in their place. Now the very next batch of brownies to come out of the kitchen would be harmless. The Allbright student body was about to go off its meds.

That was a great start, but Brooklyn still needed to get into the storeroom to do the heavy switching out. And so, on Tuesday he told Reuben that the kitchen staff was complaining about his backpack, that it was in their way. Brooklyn wondered if he could keep it in the storeroom.

Reuben unlocked the door, stood there while Brooklyn put his backpack inside, and then locked it again. Brooklyn was starting to worry. If he didn't get into the storeroom that day, he had only three days left to switch out three backpacks full of brownie mix. If something happened on just one of those days so that he couldn't get into the store-room, he'd have to come back for a *third* week of work duty so he could finish. Reuben might start asking questions.

But later that afternoon his luck turned. Reuben set him to filling salt and pepper shakers. That gave him enough time alone in there to switch out the first load of brownie mix.

Wednesday, however, did not go so well. Reuben just stood with the door open while Brooklyn dropped off his backpack. He did the same at the end of the day. Nothing accomplished.

By Thursday Brooklyn was getting desperate. He suggested to Reuben that the storeroom shelves could use some tidying.

"What's the matter with 'em?" Reuben asked.

"When I was filling up the canisters, I noticed that things seem spread out a lot. You could fit more supplies in there if you just straightened things up a little. Plus the shelves are pretty dusty."

Reuben shrugged. "Sure," he said. "Why not? I'm runnin' out of jobs for you to do anyway." And so the second backpack full of ChokoDream was successfully exchanged for Recipe Variant II. Only one more day and he'd be done.

On Friday he told Reuben that he wasn't finished tidying the storeroom, and Reuben said fine, go to it. Brooklyn pulled the door almost shut, dragged out the box of brownie mix, and went to work switching the bags. He was feeling intense relief. It would all be over in a matter of minutes.

This is always the point in any story where something inevitably goes wrong. Maybe you get too confident and let your guard down. Or maybe by then you've done one too many suspicious things. Anyway, there he was, squatting on the floor, with bags of Recipe Variant II scattered all around him, pulling bags of commercial brownie mix out of his backpack and arranging them neatly in the bottom of the box, when a voice exploded behind him.

"What in *tarnation* do you think you're doing?"

Reuben was standing at the half-open door, mad as a wet cat. As Brooklyn described it to us later, he felt electric waves of terror coursing through his body. For a minute, he said, he absolutely couldn't breathe.

"Did you hear what I asked you?"

"Yes, sir."

"What. Are. You. *Doing*?"

"I'm, um, tidying the bags of brownie mix?"

"Do I look stupid?"

"No. No you don't. Not stupid at all."

"Then let's try it again. *What in tarnation do you think you're doing?*"

"I can explain, but it's kind of complicated."

"I got all afternoon," Reuben said, and his voice was cold and hard.

There was nothing to do but tell the truth.

Brooklyn started with Cal's discovery, told about the Hopkins lab and the three compounds Prescott had found in the brownie mix. Detail by detail, he laid the whole thing out.

"So that's it," he said finally, having run out of things to say.

"Is this some kind of practical joke? You really expect me to believe a story like that?"

"No, and yes," Brooklyn said. "It's not a joke. And at least I hope you believe it, because it's pretty important that you do. Strike that. It's extremely important."

Reuben stared at him inscrutably. Brooklyn didn't have a clue as to what he was thinking.

"Okay, how about this," Brooklyn said. "Have you ever noticed how incredibly docile and well-behaved and pleasant and attractive the Allbright students are? Do you know any other group of kids like that?"

"Sure they're different; they're rich and they're smart."

"Nah, that's not it. Rich, smart kids can be just as mean and messy and lazy and rude as any other kids. A lot of them are worse, because they feel entitled. But the Allbright students are in a whole other league; they're so perfect it's creepy."

"All of 'em except for you, huh? Seems like you cornered the market on trouble."

"I wasn't really in trouble. I just made that up so I could get in here and switch out the brownie mix."

"What a surprise," Reuben said dryly.

"C'mon, think about it! Why would I go to the trouble of coming in here and working in the kitchen for two weeks, cleaning out garbage cans, and wiping down counters, and sweeping floors, just so I could load bags of ChokoDream brownie mix in and take the Recipe Variant II out? What possible motive could I have for doing that?"

Reuben didn't say anything for a pretty long time. He was nodding his head in a thoughtful sort of way. "I always kind of wondered about that 'Recipe Variant' business," he said finally. "And I sure never heard of a school pushing brownies on their kids the way they do here. And then, you know, everything else in the kitchen comes from a commercial supplier—except for the brownie mix. Dr. Gallow, he brings that in personally, every month, in the trunk of his car."

"You're kidding me!"

"No, I'm not."

More silent staring.

"So, what's your long-range plan, kid? You gonna keep coming in here every month with some cock-and-bull story about getting in trouble so you can switch out the brownie mix?"

Brooklyn took a deep breath. "We haven't actually

gotten that far. First we just need to see what happens when the whole school isn't being medicated. And while we're waiting on that—it'll take a couple of weeks at least—my science-nerd friend is going to finish analyzing the compounds. By next weekend, maybe we'll have the formulas and everything. Then we'll decide what to do."

"You're gonna shut down this school, aren't you? Lose me my job."

"I don't know. Probably."

"It's too bad, you know? And not just because of my job, either. It seems like they got a really fine place here, for smart kids like you. But if they're doing what you say they're doing, this school's gonna close."

"Oh, they're doing it, all right. But you've got a point. It would be a shame to throw the cup out with the tea bag."

"Cup with the *what*?"

"Like 'the baby with the bathwater,' only I like to come up with my own metaphors."

"Sheeeesh!"

"Look, Reuben, I need to know if you're going to keep this to yourself till we've decided what we're going to do about it. If you're still not convinced, you can take one of these bags home with you and make up a batch. Eat one a day for about two weeks and see what happens. Would you do that, at least, before you go telling anybody?"

"Don't need to. I believe you. That's story's too darn weird to make up. I'll keep your secret."

"Wow, thanks!"

"And Brooklyn?"

"Yeah?"

"You got a friend here. In case you need one."

13

We had now accomplished two important things.

First, thanks to Brooklyn the Allbright students were no longer ingesting three previously unknown compounds along with their daily brownies. We were already seeing some pretty interesting changes on campus.

And second, thanks to Prescott we now knew what those three compounds were—though I have to say I was sort of disappointed when he showed us the formulas. They had these totally weird, unpronounceable names that didn't make sense to a normal person. I mean, if he'd told us there was arsenic in the brownies, say, or antifreeze, now that would mean something. But 2,4-dimethyloxy-5-ethoxyamatronase-doodly-doot? Who could make sense of that?

A biochemist could, Prescott said. We decided to take his word for it.

Since they were brand-new compounds, his new pal over at the Hopkins lab suggested that it might be interesting to see if anybody had applied for a patent on them. She promised to look into it but warned Prescott not to hold his breath—the patent office, like most government agencies, was notoriously slow. Still, if it turned out that there *was* an application and it had Dr. Gallow's name on it, then that would be evidence with a capital E.

Meanwhile, we still had a long way to go. We needed stronger proof against Dr. Gallow, proof that he had personally and intentionally put those compounds into the brownie mix—that the wind hadn't blown them in, for example, or his evil lab assistant wasn't actually the culprit. We also had to find out who, if anyone, was helping Dr. Gallow. Was this a one-man deal or a huge conspiracy? Bottom line, we needed a whole lot more information.

Where better to find it than in Dr. Bodempfedder's office?

The administration office was usually open till five, but on Thursdays Dr. Bodempfedder left early for her weekly four-fifteen appointment with her manicurist. Ms. Lollyheart had mentioned this to Cal one time, when she came by the infirmary to visit earlier than usual. It was a handy piece of information to have, and we took full advantage of it.

We planned our mission as carefully as a band of jewel thieves out to steal the Hope Diamond. At exactly four ten P.M.—when Dr. B was presumably pulling into the salon parking lot—we entered the building and headed straight for the headmistress's office.

Cal was the first one through the door. She went over to Ms. Lollyheart, whose desk was in the middle of the reception area, and started up a conversation. As planned, she made a point of standing over on the far right-hand side of the desk. This meant that in order to talk to her, Ms. Lollyheart had to turn to her left. Sitting in this position, she couldn't see the door to Dr. Bodempfedder's office.

Brooklyn and Prescott came in ten seconds later, carefully staying close together, so as to form a visual barrier. This was important and had to be done just right (we had even practiced it in advance) because I was creeping in behind them, trying to be invisible. We took our assigned places on the opposite side of the desk from Cal, who was doing everything in her power to keep Ms. Lollyheart's full attention. Cal was explaining, loudly and in infinite detail, this really neat idea for a community service project that we wanted to discuss with the headmistress. (Yeah, I know we'd already used that one, but there's nothing wrong with recycling. And we completely changed the details this time.)

While Cal was chattering on about our project, Brooklyn and Prescott continued to stand quietly on the far side of Ms. Lollyheart's desk, acting as human shields in case she unexpectedly turned around. "So," Cal said, wrapping things up, "we just wanted to run it by Dr. B and see what she thinks. Would that be all right?"

"I'm sure it would, hon," Ms. Lollyheart said, "but she's already gone for the day."

That was the signal. Now that we knew for sure that Dr. B wasn't in there—that the manicurist hadn't called in sick or something—my big moment had arrived. I tiptoed over to Dr. Bodempfedder's office, quietly opened the door, and slipped inside.

"You want to come back tomorrow?" Ms. Lollyheart was saying.

"Sure," I heard Cal say. "Do we need to make an appointment or anything?"

Ms. Lollyheart said if we came around four, that would be fine; she'd pencil us in. Cal and Brooklyn and Prescott all said good-bye. I heard the shuffling of feet and the closing of the entry door. Ms.

Lollyheart began tappety-tapping on her keyboard. Apparently she never noticed that four kids had come in, but only three had gone out.

Now that I was in there, I had to find someplace to hide, just in case Ms. Lollyheart needed to come in there to check Dr. Bodempfedder's schedule or get some paperwork out of a file or turn off the lights before locking up.

In the middle of the room on a large oriental rug sat a big antique desk with a keyboard and a flat-screen monitor on it. There was also a little sitting area over by the window with a couple of comfortable chairs and a small glass coffee table. That was it, furniture-wise. The rest of the office was pretty much bookshelves and filing cabinets, plus a couple of potted plants. Then I turned around and saw, to my huge relief, that there was a *second* door. It had to be either a closet or a bathroom.

It turned out to be a closet, a really small one, containing only a Burberry raincoat, an umbrella, a short tweed jacket, and a navy blue suit, complete with a crisp, white shirt to wear under it. (Dr. B, being a stylish lady, would naturally want to keep a change of clothes at the office, in case she spilled spaghetti sauce down the front of her jacket at lunch, or just had a really, really sweaty day.) I would have preferred a packed closet with lots of stuff to hide behind—winter coats, ski boots, tennis rackets—but any closet was better than the next-best hiding place, which was under the desk. I shut the door, scrunched down in the corner, leaned back against the wall, and waited.

A little after five I heard the door open. I heard Ms. Lollyheart come in and click off the desk lamp. Just then it occurred to me, for the first time, that the Burberry raincoat might be hers—and any minute she might open the door to get it. But I heard the reassuring jingle of keys as she locked the door, and I heaved a big sigh. Then all was silent.

Our plan was for me to wait till around six thirty, by which time it would be getting dark and everybody would be at dinner. I would then call Brooklyn on his cell phone to say that the coast was clear (he had a phone for the same reason I did—because his parents had insisted) and then tiptoe downstairs and unlock the main door.

But I realized that there was no reason for me to sit around waiting till the others got there. I could get a head start now, and it would be a lot easier, too, while there was still daylight to read by. I wouldn't have to use the mini flashlight I had in my pocket.

The filing cabinets seemed like the obvious place to start. Unfortunately, they turned out to be locked. I pulled out the pencil drawer in the center of the desk and searched for keys. I found pens and pencils, a stapler, paper clips, a miniature Kleenex box, a tin of Altoids, reading glasses, Post-it notes, and a calculator—but no keys.

Next I checked the drawers on either side. They were remarkably neat and boring. (The only unusual item I found was a pair of fleece slippers. I guess those spike heels got to be a bit much by around three in the afternoon, even for Dr. B.) But there weren't any keys in there, either. Maybe she kept them in her purse, on the ring with her car keys. Still, that seemed odd. I couldn't picture her fishing into her purse every time she wanted to open a file. No, I had a strong feeling that she would have them somewhere handy, but not too obvious.

That's when I thought of the Altoids tin. It might contain breath mints. On the other hand, it might contain something else. I opened the pencil drawer again, took out the box, and—yes! A set of tiny keys.

I didn't know what was in the cabinets, but I figured most of them were students' files. Since the drawers weren't labeled on the outside, I opened one at random, pretty much in the middle of the room.

The tabs all had names and dates on them, none earlier than the late eighties. Graduation dates, probably. I picked one, mostly because I was intrigued by the name: Juniper Manly. I discovered that Juniper had graduated in 1991. She'd lived in Aster Cottage, had gone to the Rhode Island School of Design, and was now working for an advertising agency in New York. There was a computer print-out, an e-mail from Juniper's "alumni counselor" to Dr. B, saying that Juniper was "progressing nicely." Below this, elegantly handwritten in blue ink, was the following: "a possible asset for TB's campaign?"

I wondered if there was something special about Juniper, or if the school kept track of all its gradu-ates. That was pretty hard to believe. There were so many—drawers and drawers of them! And what was that about TB's campaign?

I flipped through more M files and noticed that one had blue tape on the tab—I figured that meant he was special in some way, so I pulled it out. Saul Missner had graduated in 1988, and once again, Allbright knew where he'd gone to college (Columbia), where he was working (at the *Washington Post*), and how he was doing (just fine). There was even a folder filled with clippings of his articles. A note was stapled to his alumni counselor's e-mail, and it was in the same elegant script as before. It said that Saul should be considered for the alumni board, adding, "Saul is in a position of increasing influence and could use our guidance."

Okay, so apparently they had an army of counselors

at their beck and call. I put Saul's file back, closed and locked the drawer, and made a wild guess as to which drawer contained the S's. On the first try I got R, so I locked it and moved on to the next one.

And sure enough, there we all were, lined up together, in alphabetical order: Sharp, Frances Claire; Sharp, Joseph David; and Sharp, Zoë Elizabeth. I noted that Zoë's file had red tape on the tab. This didn't surprise me, since the school had been so anxious to get her. What *did* surprise me though, was that *my* folder was flagged too—in yellow. In that whole drawer there were only three others marked with colored tape—a blue one and two greens. Clearly, these were students they were especially interested in for some reason. But why me? I was the reject!

I took out our files and sat down on the floor by the filing cabinet. I opened mine first.

Inside I found a fat booklet with a beige cover. INVENTORY OF APTITUDES AND KNOWLEDGE, it said. My name was typed on the cover, along with the date and the name of the psychologist who had tested me. I flipped through and saw a list of all those tests I had taken. There were scores for visual perception, idea production, reasoning (inductive, analytical, and number series), spatial (structural visualization, wiggly block, paper folding), auditory (tonal memory, pitch discrimination, rhythm memory). As far as I could tell, I was average to superior in most things. That was good enough for me. I closed the book.

But the summary letter was far more interesting:

"Frances Sharp is a non-recruited applicant. (Note: her sister, Zoë Sharp, has been recruited by Dr. Martha Evergood.) Frances is above average in intelligence and generally does well in school with the exception of math, in which she is merely adequate. Her testing bears out a general strength in verbal as opposed to numerical skills. Her emotional profile suggests a child with a vivid imagination and only moderate impulse control. Though she tested quite well, she would still be in the bottom quartile of Allbright students. She is a generalist, and with the exception of her very advanced vocabulary (she is an avid reader), Franny displays no special talent." That was it. My whole self boiled down to one paragraph.

I glanced at the heading at the top of the page. Under "Recommendation," in the now familiar handwriting, it said: "Borderline. Do not admit," below which was the following: "Accepted under special arrangement (See: Zoë Elizabeth Sharp, Joseph David Sharp)."

"Cyclamen: journalism.
Mentor: Janice Kline
College: Northwestern
PD goals: Work on impulsivity,
appearance, and social skills."

This didn't tell me much that was new, other than the fact that they had decided I was going to be a journalist (I guess I should have guessed that when they'd given me Janice Kline as a mentor) and that they'd already decided what college I should go to. Though I was judged to be somewhat above average, I was not really Allbright material. They'd only accepted me so they could get Zoë. I had low impulse control, and apparently they had problems with my appearance. Thanks for noticing the imagination, though.

There was a second sheet stapled to the summary letter, so I checked it out:

Despite her borderline testing and admission under special circumstances, Frances Sharp surprised us with her performance in the Orientation exercise. Her assignment was to build the robot, and though the student doing the computer search

failed to provide her with the
instructions, Frances managed to
complete her task perfectly. That
makes her the only student, besides
TB, ever to accomplish this.

In light of her achievement, it
is likely that Frances's test scores
didn't accurately reflect her full
range of abilities, most likely due
to an unusual and complex integra-
tion of scattered individual aptitudes. Clearly, she bears watching.
Though it would be disruptive to
move her to Violet Cottage at this
point, I doubt the wisdom of too
much mediation, since we don't
really understand her profile. *Tag
with yellow.*

The letter was typed on a computer, but at the bottom, handwritten, were the initials K. B.

Well, that was satisfying: I not only had imagination, but I was also complicated! I was right up there
with the famous TB, at least where building robots
was concerned. Obviously, I was going to have to
check out the tagged files in the B drawer for anyone
with those initials—and he or she would definitely be

tagged. They had their eyes on *this* kid, big-time.

But first I wanted to finish with the Sharp family.

Now, I swear I wasn't snooping. It wasn't like reading your sister's diary or something. I just needed to know what they had in mind for us, in case it was something heinous. I closed my file and opened Zoë's.

This time I skipped the beige booklet and went straight for the summary letter.

Zoë Sharp was recommended to us by Dr. Evergood, with high praise for her apparent intuitive interpersonal and leadership skills. Though her school transcript is not impressive (she is a B student overall), and her IQ is in the low superior range, her test scores in perception/ subjectivity/socialization exceed our ability to measure them.

Personal interaction with Zoë supports our testing in this regard. She is a real standout, a beautiful child with an unstudied, natural warmth and sweetness and excep- tional magnetic personal charm. Her pronounced natural leadership abil- ity would make her an enormous

asset both to the school and to our
country. However, in our conversation she expressed a disinclination
to attend Allbright without her
siblings. We recommend they be
accepted if necessary.

As before, the recommendation section was handwritten in ink. I had to assume that the testing psy-
chologists wrote the summaries, and then
someone—almost certainly Dr. Bodempfedder—
later analyzed the data and decided what to recommend. In Zoë's case it said, "*Extraordinary*
perception/subjectivity/socialization scores. *Primary
candidate for advancement!!!* Highest recommendation. Primrose, with *specials at all levels. Tag with red.*"

Mentor: Martha Evergood.
College: probably one of the Ivies,
possibly Yale. Consider a top-tier
Southern school, such as Duke,
which might be an asset for her
politically.
PD goals: Her posture could use
some work; we might encourage a
calmer demeanor; she should upgrade
her wardrobe, though her taste
is excellent. Don't do too much,

however. She's quite wonderful the
way she is.

I put Zoë's paperwork back in the folder. I thought
it was amazing that Allbright, the school for
geniuses, valued Zoë's sweetness. And how fascinat-
ing that they actually thought she could get into
Duke or Yale (now, *there* was a stretch!). And they had
her going into politics! As my dad would say, yowza!

I did kind of see what they meant, though. Zoë
was always getting elected to things—class monitor,
student council. That's why she was at that leadership
conference in the first place, the one in D.C. where
she met Martha Evergood. I couldn't quite imagine
Zoë taking an interest in government policy and stuff
like that, but I guess they could teach it to her (maybe
that was what "specials at all levels" meant). Maybe
they thought Zoë had what Bill Clinton had, that
inborn talent for connecting to people. Actually, now
that I thought about it, she did. Holy cow! Did they
want her to run for president?

I opened J. D.'s file last. It was a lot like mine, of
course, though it wasn't tagged with colored tape.
He too was "borderline" and not recommended for
acceptance. And he too was "Accepted under special
arrangement (See: Zoë Elizabeth Sharp, Frances
Claire Sharp)." Below, where I had been assigned to

Cyclamen and a future as a journalist, J. D.'s said the following: "Testing pattern is impossible to analyze. Definite visionary."

```
No moderation advised: Violet Cottage
Mentor: Let's wait till his inclina-
tions develop more clearly
College: Wait to see what develops
PD goals: None
```

Visionaries, huh? So that's what they called kids like J. D., different, original kids with no obvious talent in a particular subject, like art or math. You couldn't predict how they'd turn out. They'd just wander along through life doing what interested them—until one day they'd decide to start Microsoft or invent an electric eyelash curler or write a book on the history of the buffalo nickel. No "moderation" was advised for them, because the school didn't have a clue how to lead them. I was pondering all this when I heard the dreaded sound of keys in a lock.

I leaped up, banging my head on the open filing cabinet. Despite the jolt of pain, I thought fast. It would take a good four seconds for me to slip our files back in the drawer and probably another five to close and lock it. Then I still needed time to run over, slip the keys back into the Altoids tin, and hide in the closet. If, as I feared, this was either Ms. Lollyheart or Dr. Bodempfedder coming back to the office, there was no time to do all of those things.

I slid the drawer closed as quietly as I could, and with the Sharp family files under my arm and the keys in my fist, I dashed across the room and into the closet. I got there a mere two seconds before the door to the office opened and the light came on.

14

I realized, sitting there in the dark on the floor of the closet, that I hadn't closed the door completely. I'd meant to, but I'd been in such a hurry and was so anxious not to make noise that I hadn't pulled it hard enough. It popped back open again. A thin shaft of light came in through the opening. Leaning forward, I realized that I could actually see through it. What I saw was Dr. Bodempfedder's back. She was sitting at her desk, punching numbers into her phone. It seemed to ring a long time before anybody answered.

"Horace," Dr. Bodempfedder said in that low, throaty voice she has. "Where are you? Through customs yet? Halfway home? Great! How was Japan?"

She rotated her chair to the side, away from the desk, so I saw her in profile now. She had her right leg crossed over her left and was bouncing it nervously.

"Sounds wonderful." Pause. "How was the speech? Did you manage that first part in Japanese?" Another pause. "Good for you! Listen, Horace—I know you must be exhausted, and I'm sorry to bother you, but I really need to talk to you tonight. Can you come over here?" Pause. "Yes, to my office."

She uncrossed her legs and sat up straighter in her chair, both feet on the floor. "Of course I understand. I wouldn't be calling you at this hour if it wasn't extremely urgent. You've been out of pocket for a week, and frankly, next time you leave the country you need to give me your contact information. Horace, we've got some real problems here."

She sighed heavily. "No. We really need to talk about it in person. There's quite a lot to say—and besides, your cell phone's not secure. I promise you, it's important."

Dr. Gallow was apparently less than thrilled at the prospect of driving over to the campus to listen to Dr. B's problems after having been on a plane for—how long did it take to get to the U.S. from Japan? Who knew? A long, long time, that's for sure. But Dr. Bodempfedder wasn't giving up.

"All right," she said, sounding exasperated. "I'll tell you this much: It seems the brownies are no longer effective . . . Yes, I mean the *entire school*." There was another brief pause and then she added, "and . . . Horace, *listen* to me! Toby Bannerman seems to have gone off the reservation." Now she leaned back in her chair and looked smug. She had gotten his attention with that one.

Toby Bannerman. TB. They had to be the same person. But why was he on a *reservation*? Or did she just mean he wasn't behaving himself somehow?

"Yes, there's quite a bit more," she said tartly. "I *told* you it was important. All right. An hour? Fine." She hung up.

Oh, wonderful! Now I was going to be stuck in that closet for umpteen million donkey's years—or at least for the hour it would take for Dr. Gallow to get there, plus probably another hour for them to have their little talk. I just prayed that Dr. Gallow wouldn't arrive wearing a coat he needed to hang up. No way could he fail to see me, sitting there on the floor. Maybe if I stood up and flattened myself against the wall, that would be better. At least I had a whole hour to decide.

As I sat there on the closet floor, going numb in the rear and needing to pee and listening to Dr. Bodempfedder pace around her office, I came up with something new to worry about: my cell phone.

What if my mom picked just this moment to give me a ring? What if Brooklyn started to wonder what was taking me so long, and called to find out?

I pictured Dr. B, stopping as she paced and cocking her head in the direction of the closet. Was that a *phone* she heard ringing in there? I imagined her opening the door, sweeping aside the Burberry raincoat, and freezing me to the wall with a killer stare. I pictured myself frantically trying to think up some explanation for why I was hiding in her closet (Oh, so sorry! I took a wrong turn and got lost in here. Then I fell asleep!).

No—it was too horrible even to consider. Unfortunately, I didn't have the option of turning off my phone, because that would make noise too. For mysterious reasons, cell-phone manufacturers have decided that people want their phones to make twinkly music when they're shutting down. I have to ask you: Why is that? So everybody in the room (or on the plane, or in the movie theater) *knows you're shutting off your cell phone*?

One good thing about imagining disasters in gory detail is that it keeps your mind occupied (in a dark and depressing sort of way) while you're waiting. And waiting. And waiting. Which is exactly what I did. Finally Dr. Gallow arrived.

"All right, what's this about the brownies?" was the first thing he said. I leaned over to peer through the opening. He was standing by the desk—a raincoat over his arm. Oh, cheez! My goose, as they say, was roasted, basted, and sliced on a platter. I was just about to get up so I could flatten myself against the far wall, when I saw Dr. Gallow turn and walk over to the sitting area, drape his coat over one chair, and sit down in the other.

Phew!

"They're not working anymore," Dr. Bodempfedder said.

Suddenly a brilliant thought popped into my head. This conversation not only promised to be really, really interesting, something I could tell the others about later if I survived this ordeal. It might also be absolutely, positively incriminating—the very proof we were looking for. I had a cell phone. Brooklyn had a cell phone. Cal had a tape recorder in her room for playing her Mandarin tapes. Slowly and carefully, I pulled out my phone and sent Brooklyn a text message: CAL TAPE RECORD MY INCOMING CALL!

"What do you mean?" Dr. Gallow was saying irritably. "Exactly how do you know they're not working?"

I waited a few seconds for Brooklyn to read the text message, then pushed speed dial, holding the phone tight to my ear in case Brooklyn answered with a loud "hello." But all I heard was the softest whisper. "Got your message. We saw the lights go on in the office, and Dr. Bodempfedder walking around in there. We're on the way to Larkspur now."

I tapped the phone twice with my fingernail to signal okay. I figured Brooklyn could hear it, but certainly Dr. B and Dr. G, who were busy talking in loud voices, would not. Then I carefully set the phone down on the floor, near the spot where the door was ajar. I tried to angle it so it would pick up the best sound.

"The kids are behaving strangely."

"You brought me here straight from the airport, after a grueling international flight, to tell me the kids are *behaving strangely*? Can you be a little more scientific about this, Katrina?"

"Achh!" she said. "No, Horace, I can't be *scientific* about this. It's not that kind of thing, but if you'd just shut up and listen, you'll see what I mean."

Dr. Gallow heaved a big sigh. They reminded me of a pair of ten-year-olds having a fight. I wondered how long it would take for Cal to reach her room and get the tape recorder going. Hurry, hurry, I thought. I hated to lose any of this!

"They've started questioning their teachers and their PD counselors. Putting their feet on the furniture. Leaving their beds unmade. Even skipping classes! And it's not just the students, either. It's the teachers, too. Honestly, walking around Allbright, you'd think you were at any other school, except that the campus is nicer. It's like nobody's moderated at all."

"Have you checked with the kitchen?"

"Of *course* I checked with the kitchen! Do you think I'm slow-witted? They're still serving brownies, Horace. Nothing has changed. It's almost like the kids' bodies have somehow adapted to the moderation chemicals, and they're no longer having any effect."

"Well, I'll take a box of Variant One over there tomorrow morning," Dr. Gallow said. "If that doesn't set things right, I can triple the dose."

"All right," said Dr. B.

"Doesn't make sense, though, if it really is campus-wide. We've got new kids who've just been on the brownies for a few months, and others who've been on them for years. They wouldn't all adapt to it in the same way at the same time."

"Maybe it was a bad batch," said Dr. B.

"No. I haven't made a new batch since October. I'm working from the exact same chemicals I used last month and the month before."

"Maybe they've gone bad."

"Katrina, excuse me, but are you a chemist?"

Dr. B admitted she was not.

"Then stop finding fault with my lab techniques."

"I'm doing nothing of the sort. I'm just searching for an explanation in a scientific way, as you suggested."

"It has to be something going on in the kitchen, a new cook who's decided to make the brownies from scratch, something like that. I'll go over tomorrow and look into it. Probably nothing to worry about."

I could hear from his voice that he was starting to feel better about the situation.

"So what's this about Toby Bannerman?" Dr. Gallow asked.

"Well, he called about the schedule for the board meeting. While we were on the phone, he mentioned that he's getting married."

"Good. Finally."

"Not to Helena, Horace. To somebody else."

"That's impossible!"

"I'm afraid not. He and Helena split up—some time ago, apparently, though this was the first I'd heard of it."

"What? Don't you have somebody keeping track of him? Good grief, Katrina, he's our top *graduate*! You didn't even know they'd broken up?"

"Of course I have somebody keeping track of him. Tom Carrolton, out there in Atlanta. His alumni counselor. He's very dutiful, sends us clippings from the paper very regularly, every time Toby makes the news. But I can't ask him to go prying into Toby's private life and report back to us about it. He'd think it was really strange. What do you want to do? Hire a private eye?"

"Maybe we should. After all the work we put into Toby, we need to know every little thing that goes on in his life. I still can't believe he broke up with Helena!"

"Well, he did. And now he's engaged to this other girl, Tamara Rodriguez. Someone he met at Yale. She's an assistant public defender there in Atlanta."

"Oh, perfect!" Dr. Gallow said bitterly. Clearly, he didn't think it was perfect at all.

"I know it's not what we'd planned for him," Dr. B said. "That we'd chosen Helena for the part. But we can't make him marry her if he doesn't want to."

"But it doesn't make *sense*, Katrina. Their psychological profiles lined up perfectly. We reinforced their relationship at every level. That much programming shouldn't unravel so easily."

"He said they moved apart in their world views."

"I *made* his world view!" Dr. Gallow shouted. "I made hers! How could they 'move apart'?"

"Don't yell at me, Horace. I'm guessing Ms. Rodriguez had something to do with changing his world view."

"But he was *programmed*! Meeting some bleeding heart in law school shouldn't have made a dent in all that work we did."

"What do you want me to say? We always knew this might happen. I told you right from the beginning: We have seven years, max, to form them. Once they graduate, they're pretty much out of our control. We can bring them back for the occasional 'seminar.' We can set them up with mentors who'll encourage them in the right direction. We can keep an eye on their progress through alumni counselors. And we can put the really important ones, like Toby, on the board of directors—get them here on campus four times a year, give them a booster dose of chemicals and reinforce their programming. We've done it all, Horace. I know you want to believe it's enough to keep them on track for life, but apparently it isn't."

There was a long silence. Then Dr. Bodempfedder spoke again. "Listen, Horace, think of how many people you know who are radically different from their parents—who left the religion they were raised in or changed their political beliefs. If parents can't determine their own children's futures, why is it so surprising that we failed to do it?"

"Parents don't have Variant Two," Dr. Gallow said, sourly. "And they have lots of outside influences to contend with—teachers, classmates, girlfriends, the whole popular-culture thing. But our kids are isolated. We're the whole shebang—and we have them for seven years, Katrina! How many director lectures do I give them over that period of time? Two hundred and fifty, something in that ballpark? How could we *possibly* lose them after all that?"

"It's true we can imprint our students better than parents can," Dr. B said. "And lots of our graduates seem to be moving along the path we set for them, at least as far as we can tell. But, Horace, Toby is an incredible young man. That's why we chose him. Maybe thinking for himself is too deep a part of his nature for him to stay programmed forever."

"Well," Dr. Gallow said, "it's not the end of the world, his breaking up with Helena. It might actually work to our advantage. A Hispanic First Lady, a Yale law grad—she could actually be an asset."

"I agree. Except there's this other thing . . ."

"Katrina, is there no end to the bad news you have for me tonight?"

"Not really. Sorry. Toby said he's decided against running for office."

"*What?*"

"He said he wants a normal life for his family. He doesn't see himself traipsing around Georgia, eating rubber chicken in tents and making promises he can't keep. That's the short version. He was quite eloquent about it, actually."

Dr. Gallow slammed his hand on the coffee table. I was amazed it didn't break.

"I was ready to run him for Congress next year! Aggggh! I don't know what we're going to do about this, Katrina—it just *kills* me! He's the best we've ever had! He was perfect! Southern, brilliant, charming, handsome, son of a famous senator. Squeaky clean. Never so much as broke the speed limit. Ohhhhh, I cannot *believe* this!"

"Horace," Dr. Bodempfedder said, "here's what I've been thinking. He'll be on campus soon for the board meeting. Ask him to stay the weekend, say we want to discuss some future plans for Allbright with him. Then maybe we could give him some of that 'Nuclear Option' you've been working on, have a nice long talk over dinner. Maybe we could get him back in line, rescue the situation."

Dr. Gallow got up and began pacing again. "It's not ready yet, the new stuff. It might not work. It might do a lot of damage."

"Horace, you had it listed with your moderation chemicals back—when was it—in 1986, '88?"

"Look, I had something I thought had potential back then, but it turned out to have some serious side effects. And to be frank, I thought we were doing fine with what we had already."

"Well, we're kind of in a time pinch here,

Horace. The board meeting is in two weeks. You might as well try it. What have you got to lose?"

"What have I got to *lose*? My perfect candidate—of age and ready to roll. The only other kid I have in Toby's league is in bloody sixth grade! I'll be using a walker before *she's* ready to run for office."

Omygosh, I thought. *He's talking about Zoë!*

"Well, then, you need to find some other way to, what is that charming phrase you use sometimes, Horace? 'Scrub his brain'?"

Oh please, oh please, oh please, oh please be recording this, I thought. Even if they caught me right that minute and smashed my cell phone and kicked me out of Allbright, we'd still have enough on tape to put those two in jail!

"Okay," Dr. Gallow said. "Get him up here for the meeting. That will give me two weeks to do some more testing. If I'm not sure I have a good product, we'll just go with Big Gun. And ask him to stay over for a day or two. Say we'll put him up at that little B and B on Summit Drive. He'll like that. We're going to have to go at him from every angle. It may take a while."

"I'll call him tomorrow."

"Okay. I'm going home," he said. "I'm dead on my feet. And, Katrina, make sure this current chaos on campus doesn't get back to the board. I've got enough on my plate already. I don't want Jonas Ford or Martha Evergood snooping around out here."

"I'll do my best."

Then, to my great relief, they both got up and walked to the door. The light went out. The keys jingled in the lock, and I was alone in the dark.

15

"Beamer?" I said. I was in my room with the door bolted, calling on my forbidden phone.

"Franny?" He was, needless to say, surprised to hear from me. We hadn't spoken since Thanksgiving.

"Yeah, it's me, believe it or not. Beamer, I'm going to be home this weekend and I really need to see you."

"Wow, Franny," he said, "gold stars to you for being the first one to call. I was so mean to you. Then I was too embarrassed to apologize. Is it too late to say I'm really, really sorry?"

"Nope. Apology accepted—especially since you were right."

"I was?"

"Yeah, unfortunately. Totally right. It's a long, sad story, though. I'll tell you all about it this weekend."

"Wow."

"Also, Beamer, I'm going to need your help with something. It has to do with what we argued about, and it's really important."

Beamer sucked air through his teeth. "I'm not going to have a whole lot of time this weekend, unfortunately. I've got to finish my project. The happiness film, remember? It's due next week and it's, like, my whole semester's grade, so I'm up to my eyeballs in editing. But I definitely want to spend *some* time with you."

"Well, let's talk about it. I'm kind of under pressure myself. Can you come over Friday night? Have dinner with us? Then we can go into the den and talk."

"Sure," he said. "And Franny—I really missed you!"

Suddenly I had tears running down my cheeks. I sniffled, then squeaked out, "Me too. See you soon," and hung up.

That Friday morning all four of us went into the office and signed up for the van to Baltimore. We had work to do.

Brooklyn was going to spend the weekend filling

yet more plastic bags with ChokoDream brownie mix (we didn't think my mom would buy our homeless-shelter story a second time). He had gone over to the kitchen the day after our visit to Dr. B's office. Reuben told him that Dr. Gallow had arrived first thing that morning with a huge box of Recipe Variant I, and hauled away all our carefully filled bags of brownie mix. Unless we brought Reuben something to put in place of the Variant I, the whole school would change back to its original state of robotic perfection in about a week.

Prescott was going to check with the lab, to see if any progress had been made on the patent search. But his main job—and it would take all weekend and then some—was to read the entire contents of Dr. Bodempfedder's hard drive.

How, you're probably wondering, did he happen to have that material in his possession? Well, it had been alarmingly easy.

After Dr. Bodempfedder left and I let the others into the Allbright administration offices that night, Cal, Brooklyn, and I started going through the files with the aid of our mini flashlights. Meanwhile, Prescott made a beeline for the computer. Now Prescott, for all his faults, is your basic law-abiding person, and he did what he did for a law-abiding reason—to bring criminals to justice. All the same, it was pretty creepy to see what a mere eighth grader was capable of, spy-wise. And everything he used was perfectly legal and for sale on the Internet.

Here's what Prescott did:

He turned off Dr. B's computer, popped a CD into the drive (it contained a Linux program called Knoppix), and plugged a 4-gigabyte jump drive into a USB port. Then he started the computer back up again and, bypassing Windows and Dr. B's password protection, went straight into the guts of her computer. He copied all her Word files—and anything else he thought looked promising—right onto his jump drive. Then he just slipped it into his pocket. Amazing!

Prescott had a *lot* of reading to do.

As for Cal and me, our job was to meet with Beamer and see if he could do something with the tape we'd made. The problem was the quality of the sound. It had been recorded on a cheap machine off my cell phone, and the phone hadn't exactly been close to the people who were talking. Bottom line: It was barely audible. We hoped Beamer could use some of the equipment at his school to take out background noise and amplify the voices.

Beamer, being the wonderful friend he is, offered to do more than we asked of him. And being the creative soul he is, he saw possibilities we never considered.

"First of all, fixing the sound won't be a problem,"

he said. "It's fussy work and it'll take some time, but I can do it. Then I'll copy it into a PowerPoint presentation, with voice-over and visuals. It'll be much more compelling that way."

"What visuals? All we have is that recording."

"Well, you said you have the formulas for those compounds. That could be a visual."

"Oh," Cal said. "We didn't bring the documents. We didn't know you'd have a way to use them. But we have more than just the formulas. We found some really good stuff in Dr. B's files."

"Well, when you get back to school, why don't you scan them and send them to me? Really, give me everything you've got. Pile on the evidence."

"Scanning those documents in the Cyclamen computer room? I don't know," I said. "Pretty scary. What if somebody saw what I was doing?"

"All right, then take digital pictures of them in the privacy of your own room and send that to me as a JPEG."

"We could," Cal said, "but I don't have a digital camera. Do you, Franny?"

"No."

"I do," Beamer said. "I'll bring it over tomorrow. You can take it with you to school for the week."

"That should work. Thanks, Beamer. We'll need to be really careful, though. I mean, we don't want a big picture of some document coming up on the screen in the computer lab, where everybody can see it."

"No, you won't need to. Just load the pictures onto the computer through a USB port, then send me all the JPEGS as e-mail attachments. Don't even bother to open them. But be very careful to delete them afterward. I'll show you how tomorrow."

"Okay."

"And why don't you take a picture of a bag of that brownie mix, too? Get some nice photos of the school. Maybe a picture of the people who are talking on the tape. Can you do that? You could probably get them out of a yearbook."

"Yeah, that's no problem. But I don't understand what you're going to do with all that stuff."

"Well, when this bottom-feeder lady is talking . . ."

"Bodempfedder."

"Yeah, her. When she's talking, we'll show her picture on the screen. When the other guy's talking, we can show his. I can pan in on the still pictures too, which makes it more visually interesting. They do it with documentaries all the time."

"Sounds good," I said.

"I can make more of a story out of it, not just some tape you're listening to. I'll start with the pictures of the school—get more than one, nice pretty ones, and make sure you get at least one shot of the building where this conversation took place. I can do a short voice-over about the founding of the school and how it was intended to train leaders, then segue into the conversation. I can even add subtitles. In case you can't understand every word they're saying, it'll be up on the screen so you can read it."

"That would be great," I said. "But it sounds complicated. Do you have time to do all that, with finishing your movie and all?"

"Sure."

"You don't either," I said. "You've got your own stuff to do."

"How about we just say I have the time and leave it at that? Okay, Franny?"

"Okay, Beamer. But you're a saint."

"I know. It's true. And I'd stay and let you worship me, but I'd better go. I can get a head start on my editing over the weekend. That'll free me up to work on the tape at school on Monday. Then as soon as you send me the documents and photos, I'll put the whole thing together. I'll see you tomorrow, though, when I come by with the camera."

As Beamer talked, I noted that his hair had grown down over his ears—not hippie-long yet, but well on its way. I remembered how I'd been so worried about that hair, afraid my friends would think he looked scuzzy—and the memory made me sick.

"Thank you, Beamer," I said, trying to keep from

crying. "You really are the best friend ever."

This was absolutely 100 percent true. As it turned out, Beamer's working on our project meant his film wasn't ready on time. Because it was late, the highest possible grade he could make was a C, when it should have been an A+. The teacher actually told him it was the best film any of his students had ever made.

I hadn't realized what helping us would cost him. But Beamer had, and he never even thought twice about it.

16

D r. Linnaeus Planck is not listed in the phone
book. Famous people never are. But we had his
address anyway. Prescott had found it on Dr. B's
computer.

We got a ride out there with Beamer's cousin
Ray, who was still living at their house and playing
in his dad's band. Lucky for us, they didn't have a
gig that Saturday.

After much heated discussion we had decided to
show Beamer's documentary (which is what it was,
and a good one, too) to Dr. Planck. We made this
decision because: (a) we were 99 percent sure he
wasn't part of the conspiracy, since none of the
creepy stuff we'd found in the files dated from

Planck's active years (it all started after he retired, when Dr. Gallow took over and Dr. Bodempfedder arrived), (b) we were nervous about going to the police ourselves, since the story we had to tell was so unbelievable, especially coming from a bunch of kids, and (c) we really wanted the Allbright board of directors to see the presentation, since they had the knowledge and the power to do whatever ought to be done. They were, after all, this incredible group of hyper-famous, extremely powerful people who were unquestionably trustworthy and totally dedicated to the school. Unfortunately, there was no way we could get into that board meeting. But Dr. Planck could.

And so, there we were, crammed into Ray's rickety car—all six of us (including Ray and Beamer). Extremely cozy.

Dr. Planck lived in Montgomery County, Maryland, near Chevy Chase. We left early Saturday afternoon, hoping to get there around five. We figured he'd be up from his afternoon nap by then (we felt sure that all old people took naps), but wouldn't have started dinner yet. Unfortunately, despite our Google Maps directions, Ray got lost. There was a construction detour and he made a wrong turn. Then we hit some traffic. It was after six by the time we arrived.

The house was grand and beautiful, as you might

expect, considering who lived there. It was a two-story, white colonial house, surrounded by big, old trees. As we pulled into the circular drive, we saw lights on downstairs.

A woman in a white uniform answered the door.

"May I help you?" she asked, clearly surprised to see us. I guess Dr. Planck didn't get a lot of visitors. She probably thought we had the wrong house, or maybe we were selling chocolate bars for our school's baseball team.

"Sorry to just show up like this," I said, the very model of politeness, "without an appointment. But we're here to speak with Dr. Planck. We're from the Allbright Academy." I waited to see if the name meant anything to her. She wasn't giving any clues, however, so I added, "Dr. Planck founded the school back in the seventies."

The nurse nodded. Apparently she knew perfectly well what the Allbright Academy was. But she still didn't invite us in.

"We were hoping we could just have a word with him," Prescott said. "It's about the school."

Before she had a chance to answer, a tall, skeletal figure came loping down the hall toward us. His white hair—so neatly combed in the pictures of him I'd seen hanging on the walls at Allbright—was wild, fanning out from his head like a halo. He was so thin that his eyes seemed to protrude from their sockets. It made me think of Egyptian mummies.

"Hide them in the bathroom!" he croaked, terror written all over his face. "Hurry! The wolves'll get 'em!" He tried to push past the nurse and scoop us into the house. He grabbed my arm, and was surprisingly strong.

"Now, Doctor P," said the nurse, prying him off of me, "you let go of that little girl, hear? There are *no* wolves. Don't I keep telling you that? They were just on the TV."

"No!" he cried, terribly agitated. "Hide them in the bathroom!"

"Honey, they don't *want* to hide in the bathroom. They're just fine where they are."

He kept turning to look behind him for any sign of the approaching wolves, clinging desperately to the nurse. There were tears in his eyes.

"'Scuse us just a minute," she said, and gently shut the door.

"Cheez," I said. "Poor guy."

"Yeah," Cal agreed. "Do you think we should leave?"

"Let's wait a minute," Brooklyn said. "Seems kind of rude to walk away. He was trying so hard to save us from those wolves and all."

We stood in the growing dark for a full ten minutes, thinking gloomy thoughts. Then the door opened again, and the nurse stepped out on the porch, pulling the door shut behind her. "He's resting now," she told us.

"Sorry," I said, though I wasn't exactly sure what I was sorry about. Mostly that this really great man, who had once won the Nobel Prize for physics, had turned into this frightened child in a shriveled-up body.

"You got something important you need to talk to him about? 'Cause if you do, he'll be a lot sharper in the morning. It's the Alzheimer's, you know. He's 'sundowning' now. Happens most every night, though not often this bad. Usually he just wants to go home—you know, to Nebraska, where he grew up. Wants to know where his mama is. But like I say, if it's important, he's more himself in the mornings."

I wondered if there was any point in going all the way out there again. I mean, how much better could he be? Even at his morning best, Dr. Planck wasn't going to be up to attending a board meeting, much less organizing an investigation or talking to the police. But, I thought, if he turned out to be a *whole* lot sharper in the mornings, we could show him the CD. Then maybe Beamer could film his shock and outrage, add it to the presentation. It was better than nothing.

"Is he really himself in the mornings?" I asked. "I mean, *really*? It's a long drive out here."

"Well, honey, that's hard to say. Some things have

stuck in his mind, you know, but some are gone for-ever. Most of the time, even when he's at his best, he doesn't remember that he ever had a wife—and they were married nearly sixty years. But he can recall his childhood like it was yesterday. And he talks about physics all the time—not that I under-stand any of it, though he seems to think I should. And he talks about that school he started. Funny that those things would be more important to him than the woman he loved."

"The mind is a curious thing," Brooklyn said. "But since it's the school we wanted to talk to him about, it's good he still remembers it. If we do come back, what would be the best time?"

"I'd say around nine. He'll have had his bath and his breakfast by then."

"We'll try to make it," Cal said. "It depends on whether we can get someone to drive us."

"Well, I need to go back inside. You kids do what you want; come or don't come, doesn't matter. We're not going anywhere."

"That didn't take long," Ray said when we got back to the car.

"It wasn't a convenient time, as it turns out," Beamer said, loading his bag of equipment into the trunk of the car.

"What—you mean you didn't have an appointment with this guy?" Ray was furious. "We drove all the way out here just on the off chance—"

"I know, Ray. Sorry. But we've got it all set up for nine o'clock tomorrow morning."

"Tomorrow morning? You expect me to drive you out here again?"

Beamer winced. "Sorry," he said. "But it's really important."

"Gaw!" said Ray, slapping the steering wheel in disgust.

"It won't take nearly as long next time," Brooklyn said. "It'll be Sunday morning, so there won't be any traffic, plus you know the way now."

"We'll have to get up at the crack of dawn," Ray groused.

"How about we take you out to dinner tonight?" Prescott said, clearly hoping to put Ray in a better frame of mind. "I know this great Italian place in D.C."

Ray seemed to think that might be all right. Eventually he calmed down. We had a delicious dinner, which Prescott paid for, and by the time we got to the cannoli, Ray had agreed to take us out to Chevy Chase the following morning.

17

The nurse from the evening before was still there. Apparently she lived in. I wondered when she managed to get any sleep.

"I'm Gloria," she said, shaking our hands as we came in. "Sorry I didn't introduce myself last night. I was a little distracted, what with the 'wolves' and all. That was a new one, I have to tell you—though he did think Yao Ming was here once, after we'd been watching a basketball game on TV. Dr. P was very annoyed that Yao left without saying good-bye."

She led us down the hall and into a beautiful sitting room. Dr. Planck, combed and neatly dressed, was settled in a wing chair, his head back and a serene expression on his face, listening to classical music. Sun was pouring through the window behind him. What a difference from our first sight of him! I couldn't get over it.

"He won't remember you were here last night," she whispered. "But he's pretty good this morning. You'll want to speak up, though. He's got the hearing aids, but he doesn't like to wear them."

Gloria introduced us to Dr. Planck, amazingly remembering all of our names. She said we were from the Allbright Academy and wanted to "have a nice little visit" with him.

"Sit down, sit down," he said, his voice hoarse and thin.

"Thank you," Prescott said, taking the chair nearest Dr. Planck while Beamer started up his laptop and inserted the CD into the drive. "Sir, we have a presentation we'd like to show you. It's about the school—about the Allbright Academy. You can watch it on a laptop. Is that okay with you?"

"Sure."

Beamer carefully placed the open computer on Dr. Planck's lap. He pushed the "up volume" arrow, then started the show. All of us except Beamer got up and stood behind Dr. Planck's chair, so we could watch it too.

Beautiful images of the campus appeared on the screen (photographed by yours truly) while

Beamer's voice began telling the history and the mission of the school—facts I had gotten straight out of an Allbright brochure. Close-ups of Dr. Gallow and Dr. Planck in their younger days came next, with a brief description of how they were co-founders of the academy. Now the camera focused in on Dr. Gallow and then pulled back out again, showing that the picture of Dr. Gallow had been part of a group photo of the Allbright administration. And standing right next to him was Dr. B, a good two inches taller than he was in her high heels, and looking stunning as always. Once again the camera came in closer. Now we just saw their two faces.

"The following conversation took place . . ." Beamer's narration set the scene, leaving out any mention of a certain eighth grader hiding in the closet with a cell phone.

The voices began, in mid-argument, from the moment Cal had started the recorder. Beamer had done an amazing job with the sound. It was mostly very clear, but he had put subtitles in to make sure you didn't miss a word. Dr. Planck seemed to be following it with rapt attention.

"Have you checked with the kitchen?" Dr. Gallow was saying.

"Of *course* I checked with the kitchen! Do you think I'm slow-witted? They're still serving brownies,

Horace. Nothing has changed. It's almost like the kids' bodies have somehow adapted to the moderation chemicals, and they're no longer having any effect."

At this point, Beamer had inserted a photo of a bag of brownie mix. "The brownies mentioned by Dr. Bodempfedder are served in the dining halls every day," he said in the voice-over. "When the brownie mix, labeled 'Recipe Variant II,' was analyzed by a Johns Hopkins laboratory, it was discovered that three chemical compounds had been added to it."

Now the lab results came up on the screen, while Prescott's voice read the three formulas (Beamer had been afraid he'd botch those long names, and who can blame him?).

Dr. Planck leaned forward with intense interest.

We had argued about putting the formulas into the presentation. They would be meaningless to most people, I said, and it might break the spell of the narrative. But Prescott had argued strongly for including them. Dr. Planck was our target audience, and he was very definitely not "most people."

"Yeah," I'd said, "but he's been retired for years. I'll bet he's forgotten all that stuff."

"No," Prescott had said. "Absolutely not. Numbers and formulas are like a second language to scientists. Dr. Planck won't have forgotten."

And apparently he'd been right. The old man might have been gazing at pictures of his first sweetheart. Maybe, I thought, numbers and formulas really *had* been his first sweetheart. Maybe that's how he'd gotten to be so good at science that he won a Nobel Prize.

Now we returned to the recorded conversation.

"Well, I'll take a box of Variant One over there tomorrow morning," Dr. Gallow was saying. "If that doesn't set things right, I can triple the dose."

"All right," said Dr. B.

Once again we broke away from the conversation, and up on the screen came our first "smoking gun": a document we'd found in Dr. Bodempfedder's files, in a folder marked "HG." We had assumed HG referred to Horace Gallow, and sure enough, it turned out to be a treasure trove of letters (and later, printed e-mails) that he had sent her. This one was dated 1986.

There was a cover letter attached to the document with a paper clip. In it, Dr. Gallow wrote that he had finally come up with a "strong moderation plan" that he felt would "meet the school's needs" far better than their "current system" (whatever that was). He apologized wryly for the "whimsical names" he had given his new compounds and asked for her thoughts on the overall concept and "its potential as a tool for successful programming."

The document was titled "Moderation/Modification Delivery Products," and it went like this:

1. Recipe Variant I (brownie mix)—for use during the first two weeks of school and after long vacations (strong, starter dose). Contents:

(a) *Golden Glow*—general mood enhancement. The effect is one of overall well-being, promoting cheerfulness and counteracting both depression and elation. It should work extraordinarily well to moderate adolescent mood swings, producing a mellow, happy child. Very slight blue visual effects; this cannot be avoided.

(b) *Straight and Narrow*—behavior moderation (mitigates tendencies to restlessness, inattention, impulsivity, etc.) At the same time, Straight and Narrow provides remarkable intellectual enhancement, orderly thought, and very focused concentration. When combined with Golden Glow, the result is adult-like behavior, in the best possible sense. To prevent sleeplessness, it should probably not be given in the afternoon.

(c) *Big Brother*—causes profound receptiveness to any outside influence and/or programming. This is an extremely powerful drug, but it only stays in the system for a short time. Programming sessions will be most effective 1–3 hours after ingestion. Consequently, I suggest you arrange for the dining halls to serve the brownies at lunch, rather than at dinner (see above note about sleeplessness), and to maximize programming potential, I plan to move my weekly class lectures to the early afternoon, right after lunch, rather than first thing in the morning as is currently scheduled. The same goes for students' meetings with their PD counselors and my in-service presentations to teachers, counselors, and staff.

2. **Recipe Variant II (brownie mix)**—for use during the remainder of the school year (normal, maintenance dose of Recipe Variant I).

3. **Recipe Variant III (brownie mix)**—for use over the shorter school holidays. We will send baskets home with the students. Variant III does not contain Big Brother (obviously, this is not a drug we want our students taking when they are away from campus, since we cannot control the influences to which they will become vulnerable, especially that of their parents and friends, which might run counter to our efforts at programming them

at school). But we can still maintain and reinforce the improvements brought about by Golden Glow and Straight and Narrow. It is hoped that eventually, these behaviors will be so ingrained as to be part of their persona.

4. Multivitamins (standard over-the-counter daily vitamins)—to be given to current students for daily use during the school year. Not really necessary from a nutritional standpoint, as our school menu is healthy and well balanced; the actual purpose is to get them accustomed to taking a pill a day (see below).

5. Multivitamins (mood/behavior moderation, no outside modification effect; identical capsule to the over-the-counter vitamins)—for use by all students during summer vacation (those who don't enroll in the suggested summer program). They contain Golden Glow and Straight and Narrow only. Like Recipe Variant III, they will reinforce their improved behavior patterns and enhance learning over the summer.

6. *Big Gun* (elixir)—to be used under special circumstances to strongly reinforce our programming. This is a much stronger variation of Big Brother. It has some unfortunate auditory side effects (especially an annoying, high-pitched, mosquito-like sound that comes and goes) and so I have rejected it for daily use.

7. *Nuclear Option* (**elixir**)—still under development. I hope this could be even more powerful than Big Gun, but without the problematic side effects. This would be the ultimate programming tool for special circumstances. There is even some possibility that it could be used on a daily basis, replacing Big Brother.

Under these headings he had also listed the formulas. We had decided to leave the page up on the screen for a fairly long time so that Dr. Planck could read them if he wanted to. Apparently he did—he was leaning close to the screen again, squinting, following as he read with his finger.

Then it was back to the conversation again.

"So what's this about Toby Bannerman?" Dr. Gallow asked.

"Well, he called about the schedule for the board meeting. While we were on the phone, he mentioned that he's getting married."

Up came a picture of Toby, taken from the yearbook—a handsome dude, I had to admit. Then, as they discussed his alumni counselor, the possibility of hiring a detective to keep an eye on him, and the change in his marriage plans, we saw newspaper clippings about his various accomplishments over the years. Brooklyn had found them in Toby's file in Dr. B's office that night and made photocopies of them. They definitely added to the presentation.

Toward the end of the tape, where Dr. Gallow says, "It's not really ready yet, the new stuff. It might not work. It might do a lot of damage," Beamer had inserted the Moderation/Modification Delivery Products list again. Slowly the camera panned down to the last item, *"Nuclear Option (elixir)—still under development."*

Finally the taped conversation ended and we returned to the beautiful Allbright campus. Beamer wrapped it up with feeling:

The Allbright Academy: the brainchild of two great scientists with a dream, a remarkable school where future leaders of America are given the finest possible education, preparing them to take their places on the world stage. (Rising music and a video image of an American flag flapping in the breeze.)

What has become of it now?

18

Beamer took the laptop from Dr. Planck and we all stood there, breathlessly waiting for his reaction.

He smiled. "Excellent work," he croaked. We all relaxed. "Excellent."

"Sir," Beamer said, "would you mind if I videotaped you discussing the presentation? For my film class?"

He waved a papery hand in the air. "Not at all," he said. "I've been on TV before," he added. "Many times."

"I'm sure you have," Beamer said, opening his tripod in record time and setting up his camera. "The light's great," he added to no one in particu-

lar, "the way it hits the side of his face." Then he pressed the start button. "Okay."

"So, Dr. Planck," Prescott began, "you have just watched our presentation. Can you tell us what you thought of it?"

"You did an excellent job," he said, nodding enthusiastically.

"I mean, about the information it revealed? About the chemicals being given to the students at the Allbright Academy to change their personalities and make them docile and accepting of authority?"

"Well, Horace is a brilliant chemist. I never doubted he could do it."

Prescott stood there, his mouth hanging open, unable to say anything more. We had clearly miscalculated, where Dr. Planck was concerned. All the same, we might have just stumbled on a gold mine.

"Dr. Planck," I said, stepping in as interviewer, since Prescott seemed down for the count, "did you help develop the compounds?"

"Oh, goodness, no! I'm a physicist, not a chemist. That's Horace's department. He won the Nobel Prize, you know."

"Yes. We were aware of that."

"I did too, of course."

"Yes," I said again. "And congratulations on that. But would you mind telling us—was it part of the original plan for Dr. Gallow to come up with chemicals that would be, um, useful at the school? Or was that something he came up with later?"

"Of *course* it was part of the plan," Dr. Planck snapped. "And it wasn't his idea, either, though he may like to take credit for it. It was mine. That's why I went to Horace in the first place. I needed a top chemist."

"But, sir—Dr. Planck—I was just wondering. With handpicked students, and all of them so smart and everything, why did you need the chemicals?"

"To control them—help us form their characters, and their ideas, and their habits, and their world views. I've explained this to you a thousand times, Clara."

"Uh, sir—actually, I'm not . . ." Beamer poked me in the back and I shut up.

"Form their characters for what purpose, exactly?" Brooklyn asked.

"To save our country from democracy, which, as you know, doesn't work."

"Really!" I said, feeling like Alice after she fell down the rabbit hole.

"A ridiculous system. Everybody gets a vote, no matter who they are. Stupid people, uneducated people, crazy people, criminals, half-wits. The moderately stupid people vote their narrow self-interest. The *really* stupid people don't even know what their self-interest is, so they just vote for the handsome guy with the good teeth or the candidate with the expensive ads. These people don't know squat, of course, so they choose idiots to represent them, and those idiots just pander to the stupid ideas of the stupid people, in order to get reelected. That's how we run this country. It's abysmal, really."

I was feeling this strange sense of déjà vu. Where had I heard that stuff before? And then it hit me: Dr. Gallow's lectures! Of course, he expressed his ideas differently. Very elegant, very delicate, making scholarly references to the birth of democracy in Classical Greece, and how the voting population of Athens was only about the size of Lufkin, Texas, so it was manageable back then. Telling us how impractical it was nowadays, in a country the size of America, to manage even a representative form of democracy. And we just followed him down that philosophical path without realizing where we were headed.

Dr. Planck, on the other hand, practically hit you over the head with it. No pussyfooting around, no mincing of words—he gave you the Allbright agenda in all its ugliness. As my dad likes to say, he "put it out there where the cows could get at it." I was momentarily speechless with horror.

"Excuse me," Cal said. "I don't mean to sound dense here, but what's the connection between smart kids at Allbright and the, um, problems you have with democracy?"

"Well, we can't overthrow the government!" he said. "Wish we could, but I honestly don't think it can be done. So we have to do an end run. It's the only way."

"An end run?"

"Recruit the top students, educate them to perfection, form their ideas, and send them out into the world to hold key positions."

"You mean, like president?" I asked.

"Not just president. We need people in science and technology, in economics and business, to build our economy. We need policy and government people, mostly behind the scenes, making the right decisions at the various agencies. Journalists and writers to help form public opinion—and, of course, politicians at the local and national level. One by one, our graduates are going to replace those idiots in Washington. No more peanut farmers like that yokel we've got in the White House now."

"Peanut farmer . . . are you talking about Jimmy Carter?" I was thunderstruck.

"How many peanut farmers do we *have* in the White House?"

"But . . . !" I said, about to point out that Jimmy Carter was ancient history, presidentially speaking, only Beamer poked me in the back again and I came to my senses. We were trying to get Dr. Planck to talk, and he might get really upset if I told him he was drastically out of date as to who was currently in the White House.

"Please go on, sir," Beamer said. "Sorry for the interruption."

"Where was I?" Dr. Planck ran his fingers through his hair, giving it the wild look of the night before. "What was I talking about?"

"The failure of democracy," I said helpfully. "Replacing peanut farmers." When he gave me a blank look, I added, "The Allbright Academy."

But he just dismissed me with an irritated wave. "Enough, Clara," he said. "I'm tired. Tell Mother I want some tea." Then, looking at me through half-closed eyes, he added, "And send your little friends home."

"Did you get what you needed?" Gloria asked as she walked us to the door.

"Pretty much," I said. "But, I have to ask, who's Clara?"

"His sister," Gloria said. "She died, I don't know, in the late sixties, I'd guess. He talks to her a lot."

"Ah," I said.

"Like I told you, he's confused about things, but I've worked in this house for more than twenty-five years, since before he got the Alzheimer's and all, and in lots of ways he hasn't changed a bit.

Still his own, true self."

"'Stupid people?'"

She nodded. "You got it. Stupid people. Need to have a Ph.D. to have an opinion. He can't understand why they let folks like me vote."

"Wow," I said, as she led us to the front door. "I'm amazed you stayed on."

She shrugged. "Pay's good. And Beatrice, his wife, she was a real sweet lady. Now he's alone and he's old and helpless. It doesn't hurt me to hear those things. I know which of us is smart and which of us is crazy." She looked away, with this private smile on her face. Then, almost under her breath, she added bitterly, "The *great man*."

19

"Well, that was a total bust," Cal said as we drove away from the house. "Not to mention really, really depressing."

"Depressing, yes," Prescott said, "but not a bust. That interview was a prime piece of evidence. We can get Spielberg, here, to add it to the presentation."

I winced. Beamer rolled his eyes.

"Prescott," I said, "his name is Beamer and he is doing us a huge favor. He's not some servant you can order around."

Beamer touched my arm. "Doesn't bother me," he said.

"Well, it should."

Prescott, who was sitting up front with Cal and Ray, turned around and looked at me, puzzled. "What?"

"I liked you better on the brownies," I muttered.

"Um, guys," Brooklyn said, "can we try to stay on track? Prescott is right. The visit wasn't a complete disaster. I also agree that, if Beamer is very *kindly* willing to help us a little bit more, by adding the interview to the presentation, it'll be that much more powerful. I'd leave out the part about Jimmy Carter, maybe. Some of that other stuff."

"See, Prescott?" I said. "*That's* how it's done. Same content, much better result."

Prescott didn't say a word.

"Guys," Cal said, "we still don't have a plan. We can't get it to the board without Dr. Planck."

"How about Martha Evergood?" I suggested.

"Yeah," Brooklyn said. "That's a good possibility."

Then Prescott turned around, leaned his chin on his arm, and gave us a thoughtful look. "Let's reboot this whole thing," he said. "Start over. Wipe out the old ideas. Why are we so focused on taking this to the board of directors' meeting? Maybe it's time to take it to the police."

"Police?" This from Ray, who until then had only been half listening to our conversation. But *police* had been the magic word. "What the hay are you kids up to?"

"Well, it's sort of complicated," Beamer explained. "The school they go to is doing some illegal things. We thought the guy we just went to visit would help us fix the situation, only he turned out to be the bad guy himself. So we're looking into other options."

"I thought you were doing this for a school assignment," Ray said, still grappling with the new concept.

"I lied."

Ray had to think about that for a while. He was clearly not the swiftest minnow in the stream. This new twist was apparently more than he could absorb.

"People?" Prescott said, finally. "Police?"

Everybody turned to look at Brooklyn, who shook his head. "No way. Not my mom. Sorry. The, um, hacking, and the breaking and entering, and the lying—I'm not ready to lay all that out for her just yet. Preferably never."

"Some other police officer, then."

"Fine, just so long as the officer isn't related to me and living in my house."

"I don't know," Cal said. "They're going to think we're crazy."

"Not once they see the evidence." Prescott seemed very sure of this.

"All right," she said, not entirely convinced. "Whatever."

"Then let me plug the interview into the presentation first," Beamer said. "I'll just pull key sections out, so he won't seem so senile. It'll take about an hour, probably less. You guys can wait at my house while I do it, then we can go straight to the police station from there. I'm sure Ray will be glad to drive us. Right, Ray?" He leaned forward and patted Ray on the shoulder. His only response was a shrug. "What time do you have to catch the van back to Allbright?"

"Five thirty. But we need to go home first and pick up our stuff."

"That gives us plenty of time. Is everybody okay with the plan?"

Everybody was.

The officer behind the desk looked weary. In fact, everybody in the station house looked weary. I guess fighting crime is an exhausting job. Or maybe the ceaseless sound of ringing phones had worn them to a nub.

"What can I do for you folks?" the officer asked.

"We're here to report a crime," Prescott answered.

"And what sort of crime would that be?"

We all looked at one another. How, exactly, should we describe it?

"Giving drugs to children without their permission?" I suggested.

"What kind of drugs, exactly?"

"They're previously unknown compounds," Prescott said. I knew right away that this was the wrong thing to say. It came out sounding way too goofy.

"We, uh, have everything here on the computer," Beamer said, indicating his laptop. "All the evidence."

"*Evidence*, huh?" The officer raised his eyebrows and gave us an amused look, the one he probably saved for wackos who think there are aliens living in their toothpaste tubes. "Evidence is always good. If you'll fill out this form, please . . ."

We went over and sat on some plastic chairs and filled out the form. Cal has really nice handwriting, so we gave her the job, using Beamer's laptop as a desk, and we discussed every question as a group. It took forever. Finally we brought the form back to the man at the desk. He glanced over it, apparently focusing mostly on the description of the crime.

"This is a joke, right?"

"No, sir."

"The school is putting drugs in your *brownies*?"

How I wished it had been anything but brownies—they made the whole thing sound so silly.

"If you'll take a look at our presentation," Prescott said, "you'll see we had the brownies analyzed by a

Hopkins lab. There were three separate compounds that had been added."

I was desperately hoping Prescott wouldn't say anything about programming and the fall of democracy. We sounded nuts enough already.

"*You* had the brownies analyzed by a Hopkins lab?"

"Yes, I did. My mother works there."

"Ah. Your mother works there. Very handy. Well, we'll look into it."

"That's all?"

"We'll look into it."

"But don't you want to see the presentation?"

"We'll give you a call."

"See?" Cal said, as we walked back to Ray's car. "That's exactly what I was afraid of."

"It's a tough sell," Brooklyn admitted, "a story like that. Would *you* believe it if somebody laid it on you?"

"Of course not," Cal said. "Which is why—"

"Give it a rest," Prescott said. "You were right. It's over. What now?"

"Can't we just leave it up to the police," I suggested, "now that we've already gone in there and humiliated ourselves?"

"They're not going to do anything," Cal said. "That guy thought it was a joke."

"But aren't they required by law to look into all complaints, especially when the welfare of children is involved?"

"Yeah, they probably are," Brooklyn agreed. "And I can just see it now: An officer walks into Dr. B's office. 'Excuse me, ma'am, but there has been a complaint filed by, um, Brooklyn Offloffalof, Frances Sharp, Calpurnia Fiorello, and, um, Prescott Bottomy the Third.'"

"I didn't put 'the Third' on the form!"

"'They claim you are, um, putting *drugs* in the brownies out here. Sorry, ma'am, but we have to check these things out. . . .'"

"Yeah," I said. "That's exactly how it will go. And then Dr. B will explain that we are all a bunch of goofballs, always playing practical jokes, and she'll seem so refined and proper and beautiful and smart that he'll be eating out of her hand. Then the minute he leaves, we're toast."

"I hate to say this, but we need an adult to help us," Brooklyn said. "Somebody the police won't laugh at. Which brings us back to Martha Evergood. She's powerful, she's connected to the school, and I bet we can get to her through Zoë. Dr. Evergood was the one who recommended Zoë for Allbright in the first place, right? And she's really involved with the kids she mentors."

"What about Ms. Lollyheart?" Cal suggested.

"Doesn't she work for the bottom feeder?" Beamer asked.

"She's a secretary. She doesn't make decisions or anything. She's just this really amazing person who's made the school her whole life."

"Yeah," Brooklyn said, "I like her too. But it still makes me nervous. She works so closely with Dr. B and they made her orientation leader and everything. The school depends on her for a lot of important stuff."

"Well, I still think we can trust her," Cal said.

"All right," Brooklyn agreed. "She's on the short list. Plus, there's Reuben."

"What can *he* do?" Prescott said with a sneer in his voice. "He works in the kitchen."

Brooklyn glared at Prescott with squinty eyes. "Yeah, and he risked his job switching out that last batch of brownies for us. Hauled the bad ones away and has them stored in his garage."

"Calm down. I didn't mean anything negative or racist, Brooklyn. I just don't think he has, you know, influence or anything. Not like a former secretary of state."

"I'm just saying that he knows what's going on, and he's promised to help us. You never know."

"All right, all right!" Prescott put his hands up in mock defense. "He's on the list."

"Okay," I said. "We've got three people we think

216

we can trust, but if you want my opinion, I still think Dr. Evergood is the best bet. At least let's try her first. Want me to call Zoë?"

Silent nods all around.

"Wow," Zoë said, when the presentation was over. "That's . . . absolutely . . . horrifying! And it explains so much—why I felt different after I got here. Smarter, you know? And then when I stopped eating the brownies because you told me to, after a while I started to feel normal again."

"I don't feel different," said J. D., whom Zoë had insisted on bringing along. "I never did."

"That's because you're in this special category—what they call visionaries. They put you all in Violet Cottage and left you alone, to develop in your own unique ways. No brownies, no PD."

"That so *fits!*" he said excitedly. "The kids in Violet seemed like the only normal people on campus. It was really starting to weird me out, all these creepy, perfect kids. I felt like I was in an institution or something."

"And Zoë—I'm not sure if you caught that reference, during the taped conversation? 'The only other kid in Toby's league is in sixth grade'? That's you. They've been grooming *you* to be president."

"Of what?"

"Of the United States!"

"No!"

"Yes! You're, like, their discovery of the decade!"

Her mouth hung open. For a minute she couldn't speak.

"So, what are you going to do?" J. D. asked. "Tell the police?"

I sighed. "We already tried that. They thought we were hilarious. We're guessing that either they won't do anything, or they'll do just enough to warn Dr. Gallow and Dr. Bodempfedder that we're onto them, and get us in trouble."

"Guys," Cal said, "I just had a horrible thought! Even if the police *do* decide to get involved, they can't use our evidence. We got it illegally. It's tainted. They can't take it into court!"

"Yeah, they can," J. D. said.

"No, they can't," I said. "Cal's right. I saw it on *Law and Order*. If you get your evidence illegally, it's inadmissible."

"If you're a police officer and you get your evidence illegally, then yeah—that's a problem," J. D. said. "'Fruit of the poisonous tree,' they call it. But if a private citizen gives the police a tip and the police get a proper search warrant and go into the files and the computer and find the same stuff you found, it's perfectly admissible."

"How in the world did you know that?" asked Cal.

"He's a visionary, remember?" I said, feeling

suddenly very proud of my odd little brother. "He reads some very random stuff. It comes in handy sometimes."

J. D. smiled contentedly.

"Well, that's nice to know," Brooklyn said. "But unfortunately, it's not an issue. The police aren't interested in our evidence at the moment. And we need to do something pretty quick, before everything unravels—which brings us to the reason we wanted to talk to you, Zoë. We were hoping you could go to Dr. Evergood and convince her to help us."

Zoë wilted. "She's out of the country. She won't be back till Friday night. I know because she was going to take us to a reception in Washington Friday afternoon, but she had to cancel."

"Nuts!" Cal said. "I guess we'll have to wait till she gets back, but every day we wait there's a greater chance that some policeman's going to show up in Dr. B's office."

We sat there for two full minutes, feeling totally miserable. Finally Zoë broke the silence. "I have a thought," she said.

"Let's have it," Prescott said.

"Well, there's a board meeting Saturday morning."

"We know," I said.

"That's why Dr. Evergood is flying in Friday night so she can go to it. And the board members are all these really important, famous people who are willing to travel here four times a year, just because they care about the school. I say we show the evidence to them, let them take it from there."

"That was actually our plan, Zoë," Cal said. "But we can't get anywhere near those people. Dr. Evergood was our only hope, and she's not getting in till late Friday night. I can't see you calling her house at midnight to tell her all this, no matter how nice she is."

"Don't worry," Zoë said with a smile. "We're Allbright whiz kids, right? We'll figure out a way."

20

On Tuesday afternoon, during math class, there was a gentle knock on the door. Mr. Granger put his chalk down and went to open it. There stood Ms. Lollyheart, with an apologetic look on her face.

"I'm sorry, but we need to see Frances Sharp in the office." She scanned the classroom till she spotted me and made a little "come along" gesture. My heart sank. Trembling, I gathered up my books and papers and put them into my backpack. Mr. Granger stood there waiting, a bored expression on his face, while the whole class stared. I heard a giggle from the back of the room.

All I could think was that the police had made their visit. Best scenario was that they were about to

arrest Dr. Bodempfedder, and they wanted to question me as a witness. Worst scenario, the police had come and gone and I was up to my eyeballs in trouble. When I asked Ms. Lollyheart why I had been called to the office, and she said she wasn't allowed to discuss it, I knew it was going to be really, really bad.

Brooklyn and Cal were already in Dr. B's office, flanked by two security guards. I joined them and we stood there for another five or six minutes in complete, utter, horrible, painful, sickening silence, while Dr. B sat at her desk flipping through some paperwork, ignoring us completely. Ms. Lollyheart had left again, to fetch Prescott.

When he arrived, Dr. B looked up and gave the four of us an ice-cold stare.

"Cheating is not tolerated here at Allbright," she said.

"Cheating!" Prescott practically shouted. "I don't cheat! I don't *need* to cheat! I . . ."

"Please shut up, Mr. Bottomy," Dr. B said, "and don't interrupt me again. As I said, cheating is not tolerated here. There are no second chances, and you would have been expelled anyway for that alone. But breaking into my office to steal the test answers is absolutely criminal. Then going to the police to play practical jokes—I am utterly astonished. We liked you, we trusted you, and you have betrayed this school and utterly disgraced your-selves. You are expelled from Allbright as of today. I have already called your parents. They're on their way to bring you home."

"But!" we all gasped at the same time. Dr. Bodempfedder kept right on going.

"Miss Fiorello, I am aware that your father is not available to pick you up—"

"He's in Goristovia!" Cal croaked.

"Exactly. I have contacted him by e-mail, but in the meantime, it was my intention to contact Child Protective Services—"

"What!" Prescott said.

"Mr. Bottomy, I told you to be quiet. I am in no mood to listen to anything whatsoever you might have to say. Now, Miss Fiorello, Ms. Lollyheart has agreed to look after you till your father arrives. Apparently he is an old friend of hers, and she wishes to do this as a kindness to him. I have agreed. But you are not to leave her apartment, attend classes, converse with other students, or eat in the dining hall. Is that understood? If necessary, we will post a security guard outside the door."

Cal turned to look at Ms. Lollyheart, who stood in the doorway, her hands folded, staring at the floor. Then she turned back to Dr. B. "Thank you," she said. "But I didn't cheat."

"You will be escorted to your rooms by these guards. You will pack your things and stay there till your parents arrive. And I don't ever want to see any of you on this campus again. Is that clear?"

She wasn't expecting an answer. She looked back down at her papers, and the guards hustled us out.

Ms. Lollyheart took charge of Cal, and they headed off for Larkspur. One of the guards followed Prescott to Sunflower, and the other went with Brooklyn and me to Cyclamen.

Then I was in my room, shoving clothes into my laundry bag, tears running down my face. I would explain everything to my parents once we got in the car, but I couldn't bear the thought of their getting that phone call: "Your daughter is being expelled for cheating. Come pick her up right away." I was so sick with shame and embarrassment that I really thought I might throw up. I had never cheated in my life, but just to be accused of it, for my parents and classmates to believe I had done such a thing— was beyond horrible. I sat on the floor for a good ten minutes and cried.

After I calmed down enough to speak, I got my cell phone out of the drawer, went into my closet, and shut the door. First I called Zoë and left a message, telling her what had happened. "Please call Mom or Dad, whoever you can reach, and tell them it isn't true! You don't have to give them the whole story, but just say . . . whatever." I started crying again. When I finally pulled myself together, I left the same message on J. D.'s phone. Then I went back to packing.

21

B oard meetings were held on Saturday mornings at ten in the beautiful wood-paneled conference room downstairs in the administration building. At this particular meeting, in addition to Dr. Gallow and Dr. Bodempfedder, there would be seventeen of the twenty regular directors—all headliners out of *Who's Who*—plus nine members of the alumni board, successful Allbright graduates who were no slouches themselves. The parking lot would be full of limousines and, since former vice president Jonas Ford was coming, a lot of Secret Service types would be lurking about. The addition of a tall, angry-looking African-American officer from the Baltimore Police Department would go entirely unnoticed.

Ms. Lollyheart was always at these meetings, taking notes and running the PowerPoint presentations. Being a careful and conscientious person, she liked to have everything set up in advance. So, on Friday afternoons, she would take the equipment into the conference room, check to make sure the data projector hadn't blown a bulb, pull down the retractable screen, get all the trailing cords taped down so no elderly directors would trip over them, run the PowerPoint presentation through to check for glitches, and lay out the place cards that indicated where each person was to sit at the table. Then, once she was satisfied that everything was as it should be, she would turn off the equipment and lock the door.

The next morning, she would be back again early to open up the room, turn things on, make sure the kitchen staff brought in the coffee and water and sweet rolls and arranged them nicely on the serving table, and check everything out one more time.

This particular Saturday morning, however, Ms. Lollyheart did two additional things. First, she slipped a CD into the laptop. Then she went over to the handsome mahogany bookshelves that lined one wall of the conference room and added another volume to its collection of leather-bound books. She angled it slightly, so that the spine pointed directly toward the conference table, then carefully tucked the attached high-power 2.4-GHz wireless transmitter behind the other books. It was, in actual fact, a Nanny Cam, the best that money could buy, complete with an eight-hour rechargeable battery, X-vision for low-light conditions, and a wide-angle lens. Prescott had ordered it online for overnight delivery to Ms. Lollyheart's apartment at Larkspur.

Ms. Lollyheart, as you've no doubt figured out by now, was helping us. She had overheard Dr. B's conversation with the police, in which the four of us were mentioned specifically by name, followed by references to children, brownies, and chemicals. Immediately afterward she'd heard Dr. B accuse us of cheating. Knowing us as well as she did, she had the feeling something really screwy was going on. Apparently it hadn't taken her very long to figure it out.

And so, we were there too, that Saturday morning, sitting in Ms. Lollyheart's apartment. With the support of our parents, and the assistance of a secretary and a kitchen custodian (Brooklyn had called Reuben and asked him to help), we were about to bring down two criminals. That was the plan, anyway.

We'd arrived early, around five thirty, when everybody at Larkspur was still asleep (except for Cal and Ms. Lollyheart), long before Dr. Bodempfedder or Dr. Gallow would appear on campus. The night guard at Larkspur didn't know the Allbright kids at all, and he certainly didn't know who we were or that we'd been expelled. Ms. Lollyheart had simply told him she was expecting several guests, which was something of an understatement. In addition to the four of us—Brooklyn, Cal, Prescott, and me—there were Beamer, Zoë, J. D., and all of our parents (except, of course, for Cal's dad, who wouldn't arrive in the States till later that afternoon, and Brooklyn's mom, who had her own role to play). It was pretty crowded in there.

We had gathered to watch what we hoped would be the grand climax of the Allbright affair, in living color, on Ms. Lollyheart's TV, the receiving end of the Nanny Cam. There was already a blank tape in her VCR. As soon as people began to arrive and images came up on the screen, we were ready to press RECORD.

Since it's against federal law to use audio in hidden cameras, there wouldn't be any sound coming out of the television. And a whole lot of people sitting around talking without any sound wouldn't be all that informative or exciting. So, for our benefit, Ms. Lollyheart had slipped a baby monitor into her purse. The listening end was sitting next to the television. The sound quality wasn't great, but it was better than nothing. For posterity—or for possible use in court—she would also make a high-quality recording of the meeting, openly and with everyone's permission, supposedly to help her later in typing up the notes.

From around nine fifteen, when Ms. Lollyheart put the book cam in place, we could see pretty much everything that went on in the room. We watched Reuben, dressed spiffily in a white waiter's jacket, set out the beverages and breakfast rolls, while Ms. Lollyheart carefully placed a booklet, neatly bound in a blue paper cover, in front of each chair.

Two of the booklets, we knew, contained the usual material—the agenda for the meeting, the annual budget; the names of the following year's incoming students, complete with their special accomplishments and remarkable test scores; a list of the early-decision college acceptances of Allbright seniors, and lots of other inspiring stuff—the latest and greatest achievements of their current students and graduates. These two booklets were on top of the heap. We watched Ms. Lollyheart flip through them, double-checking that they were the right ones, and then place them on the table where Dr. Gallow and Dr. Bodempfedder would sit.

Everybody else got the other booklets. Though they too opened with the agenda and the budget, they also contained copies of the most damaging documents we had found: the chemical analysis of the brownies, the list of Moderation/Modification

Delivery Products, some choice quotes from Dr. Gallow, Dr. Bodempfedder, and Dr. Planck, plus Prescott's windfall discovery of just three days before. (Having been sent home, he'd had plenty of extra time to spend going through Dr. B's files, and the effort had paid off.)

We saw Ms. Lollyheart speaking softly to Reuben. He nodded and smiled. Then he finished setting up, rolled the food cart out of the room, and shut the door.

About twenty minutes later people started to arrive. The first three were graduates on the alumni board. Clearly excited by the prospect of sitting at a meeting with some of America's most famous and accomplished people, they had made it a point to get there early. Every one of them, in typical Allbright fashion, was good-looking and well dressed in a clean-cut, conservative way. As they came in, they each went over and hugged Ms. Lollyheart warmly, then took water or coffee and sat down. One woman, a wholesome-looking brunette in her thirties, picked up her booklet and started to flip through it.

"Don't!" Ms. Lollyheart said quickly. "No peeking till the meeting starts." This clearly surprised the woman, but she did as she was told.

Dr. Gallow came in next, followed by Dr. Bodempfedder. The former students jumped to their feet and went over to shake hands. They remained standing as more and more people arrived. Caroline Kelley and Michael Gates came in together, followed by Jonas Ford and Martha Evergood. It was like watching the show before the Oscars, where all the movie stars come up the red carpet and stop to chat with the press—except that the board members weren't all young and gorgeous and they weren't wearing tuxes and strapless gowns.

"I sent Dr. Evergood an e-mail *and* left a message on her answering machine," Zoë told the group. "But I don't know if she had time to check them. She got in so late last night."

"What did you say?" Mom asked, more or less into Zoë's hair. Mom had both of us in sort of a bear hug, like she had just pulled us out of the way of a speeding truck and now somehow just couldn't let go. She had tried to scoop J. D. into this embrace, but he had escaped and was, as usual, sprawled out under a piece of furniture (the coffee table), gazing at the TV.

"I just told her something very important was going to happen at the meeting and to please make sure they watched *all* of our student video, no matter what. Oh, and I said if she could order some cocoa just before the meeting started, that would really help."

Brooklyn's dad, a giant man with a full beard

and bright pink cheeks, burst into a fit of operatic laughter. "Ho, ho, ho, ho! Cocoa!" he boomed, at which we all went "Shhhhh." We were supposed to be quiet in there.

"But such an enigmatic telephone call, my dear," he said in a quieter voice. "So mysterious. What will the great lady think of it, I wonder?"

"I don't know," Zoë said, making a cute, wincing face. "That I've gone totally 'round the bend, probably."

"Hey," Brooklyn said, "check it out. Saul Roth!"

"And is that"—Prescott leaned forward to stare at the screen—"Leon Marcowicz?"

"Yes, that's Leon." This from Dr. Prescott Bottomy Jr., who, together with his wife, Dr. Arlene Clawfoot-Bottomy, was sitting in the back of the room in two of the very few chairs available. "I've met him, actually, several times. Brilliant scientist."

It was the sort of show-offy thing Prescott used to say all the time. Being around his parents made me appreciate how much progress he'd made.

"Look!" Cal said excitedly. "That's Toby. I'm sure of it."

"Yup, no question," I agreed. Mr. Future President himself. I had to admit, he did have star quality, what they call charisma. There was an easy confidence about him; he seemed genuinely modest—and kind, and warm, and funny, too. You sort of knew all that, just by looking at him. Even in a room full of famous faces, you couldn't take your eyes off him. It seemed weird that somebody so appealing should be the one they chose to undermine our whole democratic system. But then again he would be, wouldn't he? He needed that personal magic to get where they wanted him to go. After that it was just a matter of controlling him.

Poor Toby, I thought, as I watched Dr. Gallow go over and drape an arm over his shoulder in a friendly way. You have no idea what that dreadful man has planned for you and your brain!

"I wish I knew what those two are saying," I complained. It was hard to make out their conversation over the buzz of voices.

"Nothing important," Dad assured me. "Just small talk."

As it neared ten o'clock Dr. Gallow indicated that anyone who wanted coffee or water should go ahead and get it. Then, if they would please take their seats, the meeting could get started.

Just then Martha Evergood made her way over to Dr. Bodempfedder and touched her arm to get her attention. Dr. B, nearly a foot taller, had to lean way down to hear. Though Dr. Evergood's voice was lost in the background noise, we knew what she was saying: Might she have some cocoa, instead of the coffee? Would that be possible? Not too much trouble?

Yes! Dr. Evergood had gotten Zoë's message! We had one more ally in the room.

Dr. B nodded and smiled, then pulled out her cell phone and dialed the kitchen. Could they bring a pot of cocoa over to the conference room, please? Dr. Evergood smiled graciously, like the diplomat she was, and took her seat, folding her hands and looking as innocent and peaceful as your grandma in church.

Finally everyone sat down and Dr. Gallow began.

"Good morning," he said. "I want to thank you, as always, for taking time out of your busy lives to come here four times a year in support of this remarkable school."

"They don't start with the Pledge of Allegiance?" Cal said. "That's so weird."

"For a board meeting?" Dad said. "Why would they?"

"They start *everything* with the Pledge," I explained. "And 'The Star-Spangled Banner.' Allbright is very patriotic."

"Oh?" he said. "So patriotic that they want to do away with democracy?"

"Yeah, ironic, isn't it?" Brooklyn said.

Dr. Gallow was continuing with his opening remarks. Saying nothing, really, except the obvious: the board was full of really famous and important people, they were so generous to give their time to the school, and yadda, yadda, yadda. When he was done flattering the board, Ms. Lollyheart signaled to him by holding up her tape recorder. Dr. Gallow nodded. "Evelyn is going to tape the meeting, unless anyone objects. Helps her keep the minutes more accurate."

No one objected. Ms. Lollyheart set the recorder down in the middle of the table and pressed RECORD. Then, while Dr. Gallow got the meeting under way, she reached into her purse, which sat on the floor beside her chair. After some fiddling around in there, she pulled out a tissue and delicately dabbed at her nose. Ms. Lollyheart did not have allergies or a cold. She didn't really need the tissue. It had just been an excuse to reach into her purse and press the speed-dial button on her cell phone.

Outside, just down the hall, Reuben was waiting with a silver tray and a pot of lukewarm cocoa. He had Brooklyn's cell phone in his pocket, set on VIBRATE. When it went off, that was the signal for him to walk down the hall to the conference room and knock on the door.

"Evelyn, would you get that please?" said Dr. B. Ms. Lollyheart got up and opened the door. Reuben came in with the tray, laid an empty cup in front of the former secretary of state, and was about to pour cocoa into it. But somehow he lost his balance, and the contents of the pot went not into the cup but on the table—in the exact spot where Dr. Gallow and Dr. Bodempfedder were sitting. Needless to say, it got all over them. That's why it wasn't hot.

Dr. B gasped, but—I have to hand it to her—she kept her composure. Dr. Gallow, on the other hand, jumped to his feet screaming and turned on Reuben in a rage. "You idiot!" he hissed. "You're fired. Get out of here—now!"

Reuben looked appropriately horrified and hurried out of the room.

Meanwhile, Ms. Lollyheart and a couple of the younger alumni dashed over to the buffet table for napkins and did their best to clean up the mess. They even used some of the bottled water to wipe up the sticky remains of the cocoa. But nothing could be done about the ruined clothing.

"Dr. Bodempfedder," Ms. Lollyheart reminded her, "you have that navy-blue suit in your office closet."

Dr. B nodded. "I hope you'll excuse us," she said to the directors, even managing a smile. "It shouldn't take us too long to clean up."

"That is one classy lady," Cal said. "Evil, but classy."

"Shall I go ahead with the PowerPoint while we wait?" Ms. Lollyheart asked sweetly.

"Sure," grumbled Dr. Gallow on his way out.

"What do you bet *he* doesn't have a change of clothes on campus?" I said, shamelessly enjoying his misery.

As soon as they left, Ms. Lollyheart flipped off the lights and fiddled with the computer for a second. Then my photo of the Allbright campus came up on the screen and soft background music began.

"This presentation is a student piece," she said. "Made by eighth graders. I think you'll be impressed."

Everyone turned toward the screen, wearing the patient, polite expressions you might expect from brilliant, famous, accomplished people who spend their days running huge corporations or dealing with vital world issues and are then asked to sit through an eighth-grade student presentation.

They would perk up in a minute, though. I was sure of that.

We were sitting there, glued to the TV and waiting for the fireworks to begin over in the conference room, when we heard a gentle knock. We all exchanged terrified glances.

"It's Reuben," said a voice from outside the door. With a sigh of relief, Cal ran over and opened the door.

"Awesome job, dude!" Brooklyn said, and we gave him a quiet little round of applause.

"It was a pleasure," Reuben said. And you could

tell by the way he smiled that he'd definitely enjoyed pouring cocoa in Dr. Gallow's lap.

"Check it out, guys," J. D. said, pointing to the screen. "Jonas Ford—eyes as big as saucers!" He wasn't the only one. As the presentation continued, and they began to understand what it was all about, rage and alarm showed on every face.

"Stop it for a moment, Evelyn, would you please?" Vice President Ford said. She reached over and pressed PAUSE. "What *is* this? You said it was a student film."

"Yes, sir. That's correct."

"And that . . . ," he said, gesturing toward the spot where the director and headmistress had so recently been sitting, covered in cocoa, "Did you arrange that, too?"

Ms. Lollyheart nodded. "I'm afraid so. It's crucial that you see this, sir. It was the only way we could think of to make that happen."

"Let's keep going," Dr. Evergood said. "I want to watch the rest of it."

Zoë grinned. "Yay, Martha!" she said.

Ms. Lollyheart started up the presentation again. Everyone now watched with extreme interest. When the conversation switched from brownies and formulas to Toby Bannerman's future, heads turned to gaze at him in shock and sympathy. Toby was clearly thunderstruck. He leaned forward on his elbows in rapt concentration, his mouth hanging open just a little. He must have been thinking back over years and years of seemingly innocent events and what they had truly meant.

"I made his world view!" Dr. Gallow was shouting. "I made hers! How could they 'move apart'?"

"Don't yell at me, Horace. I'm guessing Ms. Rodriguez had something to do with changing his world view."

"But he was programmed! Meeting some bleeding heart in law school shouldn't have made a dent in all that work we did."

Toby lowered his face into his hands and his back heaved.

Just then Dr. Gallow came in. He had rounded up a clean jacket somewhere, and wore it buttoned up all the way—hoping, I guess, that between the jacket and the tie he could cover up most of the stains on his shirt. His trousers were still wet where he had tried to clean the cocoa off with water. It must have been embarrassing for him. Ah, but *just you wait,* I thought. Wet pants will be *nothing* compared to what's going to happen to you over the next ten minutes.

Dr. Gallow hadn't seen the PowerPoint presentation that was planned for that meeting; Dr. Bodempfedder was the one who organized them. But he knew what to expect. According to Ms. Lollyheart, they were always uplifting fluff pieces, very inspirational and never too long. They were just to get everybody in the mood and remind them what a great place Allbright was.

So now he stood there, gazing in puzzlement at something very different from what he expected, something very familiar—and we could see the realization washing over him. That was *his* picture up there. That was *his* voice. That was *his* private conversation with Dr. B, and he had no clue how it had been recorded and why it was being played for the board.

Suddenly, he lunged toward the laptop to stop the presentation. But he hadn't noticed upon entering that the policewoman who had opened the door for him (he'd assumed she was part of Jonas Ford's detail) had slipped in behind him. She now had a firm grip on his arm.

"Not so fast, Doctor," she said. With her other hand she pulled his chair out, away from the table and well out of reach of the laptop. "Sit!"

He glared at her viciously, but she gave him another yank on the arm. "I *do* mean it," she said, and you could tell that she really did. "I have handcuffs, if you want to do this the hard way."

Dr. Gallow sat.

Every face in the room was turned in Dr. Gallow's direction. These were people you didn't want to mess with, people with immense power and influence, people with a lot of pride. And the timing couldn't have been better, because just then the recorded voice of Dr. Gallow said, "And, Katrina, make sure this current chaos on campus doesn't get back to the board. I've got enough on my plate already. I don't want Jonas Ford or Martha Evergood snooping around out here."

Ford rose to his feet in outrage. Toby still had his head in his hands.

"Excuse me, please, Mr. Vice President," Ms. Lollyheart said. "There is actually quite a bit more you need to see. Then you can have your meeting and decide what you want to do about all this." Ford sat down, but he was boiling with anger.

Now Linnaeus Planck came up on the screen. It was a still picture, taken from the beginning of the interview. He looked elderly but elegant, sitting there in his wing chair, the sunlight from the window shining on his neatly combed white hair. Beamer had recorded a brief voice-over at this point, introducing him as co-founder of the school and an eminent scientist, recipient of the Nobel Prize.

For many of the board members, Planck had been their original link to the school. He was a public figure in a way Dr. Gallow had never been, and he had a lot of influential friends. In his younger days, he'd been on television a lot, had testified as a science expert before Congress, and had written a couple of bestselling books. It was due entirely to him that people like Jonas Ford and Martha Evergood had donated money to the school and given their time to recruit and mentor students and sit on its board of directors.

Heads turned. You could tell they expected something positive from him—something hopeful— just as we had. The illustrious Linnaeus Planck to the rescue. The still picture began to move. You could hear the gentle strains of Bach in the background and Prescott's voice asking that first question.

> *"So, Dr. Planck, you have just watched our presentation. Can you tell me what you thought of it?"*
>
> *"You did an excellent job."*
>
> *"I mean, about the information it revealed? About the chemicals being given the students at the Allbright Academy to change their personalities and make them docile and accepting of authority?"*
>
> *"Well, Horace is a brilliant chemist. I never doubted he could do it."*

We heard an intake of breath around the table, and

just then Dr. Bodempfedder came in, looking good as new in her navy-blue suit. As Dr. Gallow had done before her, she stood for a few seconds, gazing at the screen with a puzzled expression on her face. That was just enough time for Officer Offloffalof to pull out another chair and invite her, very firmly, to sit in it.

"Stop that!" she snapped. "Who are you? What's going on here? Horace?"

"You and Horace are going to sit right where you are and keep quiet till this little show is over," the officer said.

I could see why Brooklyn had been so careful about when to get his mom involved. She was a pretty scary lady. Dr. Bodempfedder turned and looked at this beautiful woman wearing a police uniform and a menacing gaze, and visibly recoiled.

"Like I told your friend, here, I'm not fooling around. We can do handcuffs if you want to."

"Your mom is *so* cool," Cal said.

"Yeah, she is. But you really don't want to mess with her."

The board was not paying much attention to the little face-off going on at the far end of the room. They were too busy watching, with horror, as their esteemed and trusted friend and colleague, Dr. Linnaeus Planck, revealed his true nature.

". . . Would you mind telling us—was it part of the original plan for Dr. Gallow to come up with chemicals that would be, um, useful at the school? Or was that something he came up with later?"

"Of course it was part of the plan," Dr. Planck said. *"And it wasn't his idea, either, though he may like to take credit for it. It was mine. That's why I went to Horace in the first place. I needed a top chemist."*

Dr. B, who was clueless about what had been going on while she was out of the room, leaned forward, yanked her arm away from Officer Offloffalof, and said in a loud voice, "That man is very old and has severe dementia. It's absolutely disgusting and disrespectful to film him like that. He's raving. Whose idea was this? Evelyn?"

"Please shut up, Katrina," Michael Gates said. "You're in way over your head."

Her jaw literally dropped.

"Woo hoo!" I cheered as we watched it on TV.

"Shhhh," Prescott said.

Then came our last piece of evidence, Prescott's big discovery. It was titled "Overview," and Dr. Bodempfedder had written it for Dr. Gallow, at his request, basically laying out every detail of how they created what Dr. Bodempfedder so charmingly referred to as "first-rate final products."

Allbright graduates, that is.

It was a long document, and though it was extremely creepy to read the whole thing, we'd decided to pick out only the most incriminating sections for the presentation. We included the full document in their packets for future enjoyment. I was thinking that it had been a good call; the board looked exhausted.

And so, without going into every grim detail, we showed how the teachers and PD counselors had been carefully programmed by Dr. Gallow during monthly in-service meetings (occurring right after lunch, at which Big Brother was served in the form of brownies), turning them into unwitting accomplices. But it was during Dr. Gallow's weekly lectures—also held after lunch, when students would be most vulnerable to outside influence—that the real programming work was done. Week after week, year after year, Dr. Gallow had gradually formed the students' attitudes and beliefs. In short, he was building little human guided missiles to be sent out into the world to forward his agenda.

"The Allbright experiment," Dr. Bodempfedder's memo concluded, "the result of many years of creative thought, dedicated effort, and constant fine-tuning on both our parts, can be judged an unqualified success. America is now in the capable hands of a small army of right-thinking Allbright graduates, and the future looks bright."

Jonas Ford gripped his head in his hands, completely beside himself. "This is an absolute disaster," he said.

Ms. Lollyheart closed the laptop and went over to turn the lights on.

"Ladies and gentlemen of the board, I know you have a lot to discuss," she said. "But if you'll bear with me for another thirty seconds, I need to let you know what happened after this presentation was made, in case you still have doubts as to the truthfulness of all this."

Heads nodded all around.

"Go ahead, Evelyn," Michael Gates said.

"Thank you. I mentioned earlier that this presentation was put together by students—a small group of eighth graders, to be exact. They were the ones who first discovered what was going on at Allbright. They investigated the matter and began gathering evidence. When they felt they had enough, they went to Dr. Planck, hoping he would help them. When that failed, they reported it to the police. The police, as you might imagine, didn't take the matter very seriously, but they *did* make a token visit to the campus. As a result, Dr. Bodempfedder found out that the children were onto her.

"In an effort to control the damage and make anything the kids might say about Allbright in the future seem suspect, she had them expelled on a trumped-up charge of cheating. Please believe me, they are completely innocent.

"Fortunately, one of the students has a mother in the Baltimore PD, Officer Offloffalof." Ms. Lollyheart gestured toward Brooklyn's mom, who nodded and smiled. "She brought the documents you just saw—you have copies of them in your packets, if you'll just turn to page six—she brought those documents, and the transcript of the conversation you heard, to the attention of the police once again. This time with better results. They obtained a search warrant for Dr. Bodempfedder's computer and files, as well as everything in Dr. Gallow's office and lab over at the National Science Institute. I expect they're probably over there right now, busy as little bees."

Dr. B sprung to her feet and sprinted for the door.

Officer Offloffalof made no effort to stop her. "Secret Service is out there, you know. Just scads of 'em. But go on ahead if you want to."

Dr. B paused with her hand on the knob and didn't move. She froze there, like she was playing statues.

"Why don't you just sit down, Katrina," Martha Evergood said.

Dr. B sat down.

"Is there anybody here who wishes to dispute the truth of the things you've heard this morning?" Dr. Evergood asked. "Because I, personally, am quite convinced."

"Horace?" Jonas Ford said, "Katrina? Do you have anything to say? Any possible sort of explanation?"

Dr. Gallow's expression was frightening, or at least it would be if he'd looked at *me* like that. Vice President Ford, however, didn't bat an eye.

"The results speak for themselves," he said, gesturing angrily at Toby and the other alumni board members sitting at the far end of the table. "Just look at them. Are they not far superior to any leaders we have in this country today?"

"Superior *final products*?" Saul Roth said with disgust.

"Merely a turn of phrase," Dr. Bodempfedder said. "Unfortunate, perhaps. But Horace is right. Our graduates, these perfectly educated, extremely dedicated young people, are wonderful treasures; they constitute an immeasurable gift we have given to this great nation."

"Excuse me, Katrina," Ford said, "but that is utter hogwash. And since you don't deny that you have betrayed this board, this school, and most of all its students, I suggest you save the rest of your explanation for the courtroom."

Officer Offloffalof raised her eyebrows in question. "Time to go?"

"I believe it is," Martha Evergood said.

"My pleasure, Madame Secretary. It'll take just a minute." She pulled out her phone and called for a squad car.

There was a moment of silence. Then, for the first time, Toby spoke. "Dr. Evergood? Members of the board? May I say something here?"

"Of course, Toby. Please go ahead."

"I understand that everyone here has been grossly taken advantage of, and I can just imagine how angry you are. But I am—surely you will agree—the biggest victim here. They planned to turn me into the front man for their hateful agenda. This very afternoon I was supposed to have lunch with Dr. Gallow, apparently to have my 'brain scrubbed.' You all heard it."

The others nodded sympathetically, then turned again toward Dr. Gallow, who now sat with his head resting on one hand, staring defiantly at the bookcase.

"Having said all that," Toby went on, "let me add something on a more positive note. There is one issue that hasn't been mentioned yet, and it's potentially the most disastrous aspect of this whole disastrous mess: the hundreds and hundreds of 'final products' out there, people like me and Janice and Saul." He gestured toward the other

Allbright graduates on the board. "The problem of putting the toothpaste back in the tube, as the saying goes. I just wanted to assure you that, despite their best efforts, Dr. Gallow and Dr. Bodempfedder failed. The human spirit is not that easily captured.

"When I went off to college, I carried all of Dr. Gallow's—and I am sorry to learn, Dr. Planck's—odious ideas and opinions with me, along with a thousand little 'improving' habits of behavior and manners, some of which actually proved to be helpful. But rather quickly those ideas began to fall away. I found myself evolving, learning to question authority and think for myself. My friends from Allbright, at least the ones I've kept up with, have evolved too."

Janice nodded in eager agreement.

"Yes," Saul said. "Me too."

"We truly benefited from the education we got here," Toby went on. "The rigorous curriculum, designed for our unique talents and learning styles, the incredible teachers, the mentors, the internships, the enrichment program—they were all fabulous. What a wonderful gift! But the twisted theories—once we got away from Allbright, we gradually sloughed them off. If anything, our quality education helped us do it. We are not irretrievably damaged."

"What a relief to hear you say that, Toby," Caroline Kelly said. "I desperately hope you're right. Because there are so many of you out there, so many graduates."

"I think we'll be okay. I really do."

"Toby," Martha Evergood said, "Janice, Saul, we—as representatives of this school—owe you the most profound apologies for what was done to you. It was generous beyond belief for you to be so positive about your time here. Thank you. And I must say, I'm pleased that Horace and Katrina got to hear it too. It will give them something to think about in prison—how their efforts failed. Officer Offlofalof, how long before that squad car arrives?"

"Momentito," she said, and dialed again. "Ready? Thank you." Then she dazzled the room with a beautiful smile.

"You have the right to remain silent . . . ," she began.

And over at Larkspur Cottage, students in their rooms, in the dining hall, and in the common room that Saturday morning, were astonished to hear a loud and triumphant cheer.

22

The school was shut down, but the board members stayed on to clean up the mess. We weren't around to see it, but it must have been a really big job. They had to contact everybody—the students, faculty, staff, and parents—and tell them all, one painful phone call at a time, what had been going on at Allbright.

Once the kids had gone home and the school was empty, the board began tracking down the graduates. According to Martha Evergood (who drove out to our house to personally apologize to our parents for bringing us to Allbright in the first place, and to thank us profusely for helping to nail the scumbags), Toby had been right. Beyond the astonishing degree of their success, the Allbright graduates appeared to be perfectly normal. The most encouraging discovery, Dr. Evergood said, was the great variety of their political and philosophical opinions. Each one had, in Toby's words, evolved. And ironically, they really *were* serving their country, each in his or her own unique way.

Their amazing success had so astonished the board members that once the smoke had cleared— the trial over, the former director and headmistress of Allbright in prison (Dr. Planck was judged incompetent to stand trial, but his great reputation was ruined forever), the campus and all its luxurious furnishings sold to settle the lawsuits—they voted unanimously to do the unthinkable: start another school. This one would be a day school in the D.C. area, incorporating all the positive things that had made Allbright so wonderful. And Martha Evergood would be its director.

I wish them well.

Prescott went back to his ritzy private school in Baltimore. But that summer he took an internship at a lab in the Georgetown University Medical Center in Washington, where he lived in one of the dorms. This seemed like an odd choice to me, since Hopkins had plenty of fabulous labs close to where he lived. Then Zoë shed light on the mystery.

"He wants to be near Cal," she said.

"Ah!" I said. "Of course!"

Prescott, as my dad would say, was "sweet on" Cal. Actually, I think she kind of liked him, too. Say what you will about Allbright and its personal development counselors—yeah, they went way too far with it, but in Prescott's case it had helped him a lot. He had grown almost likeable. Who would have thought it?

Cal was now living and going to school in the Virginia suburbs of D.C. Her dad had finally come to his senses. Actually, he had been in the process of resigning his position in Goristovia in favor of a stateside desk job, when bad news from Allbright started popping up in his e-mail.

Two months after he came back to make a proper home for his daughter, Mr. Fiorello married his old college friend, Ms. Lollyheart. Talk about your happy endings!

Brooklyn is now wearing his hair in a giant Afro. He says he's in his "historical period." He promised to go back to the dreadlocks eventually, because they really do suit him, but felt he needed to "explore the sixties" for a while.

When his book of poems was officially published in the spring, we gave a party for him. Now he's working on a volume of haiku. He asked if he could use the one about the tempura trees, and I said sure. He's calling it "Franny's Snow," so if this book gets published, I'll have my own little moment of fame.

As for Reuben, Martha Evergood hired him as her new driver, at three times his Allbright salary.

Zoë and J. D. and I are just glad to be home again. Mom and Dad still hover too much, but they'll get over it in time. Meanwhile, we're trying to sort out the positive things we learned at Allbright from the negative; like Toby, we're evolving. Also like Toby, we're fine.

The day after the momentous board meeting, Beamer came over to our house with his camera.

I made myself comfortable on the couch, with a fat cushion behind my head and the chenille throw wrapped cozily around me. Beamer didn't want to use natural light this time; he liked the warm glow of the pole lamp beside the couch.

Zoë and J. D. were in the den too, listening—Zoë curled up in Dad's leather chair and J. D. on the rug with his legs draped over the couch. Beamer was watching me through his camera.

"'Chapter One,'" I read. "'I Am Born. Whether I shall turn out to be the hero of my own life, or whether that station will be held by anybody else, these pages must show. To begin my life with the beginning of my life, I record that I was born (as I have been informed and believe) on a Friday, at twelve o'clock at night. It was remarked that the clock began to strike, and I began to cry, simultaneously.'"

And suddenly, like little David Copperfield, I began to cry. Not a big, loud baby's wail like David's, just a trickle of tears down my cheeks and a shaking voice as I continued to read.

How nicely he put things, I thought, old Mr. Dickens. For at that moment I knew that all of us had become the heroes of our own lives. And though I would never be a genius like Brooklyn or Prescott, I no longer thought of myself as ordinary. I had built a robot from scratch, all by myself, and together with my friends, had taken something very wrong and made it right.

I turned the page and went on reading. Beamer had stopped filming now. He sat on the floor near J. D., his arms around his legs and his chin on his knees, listening.

Outside, it began gently to rain.

A Haiku for the Allbright Academy
By Brooklyn Offloffalof

A pearl forms, slowly,
In the oyster's slick, dark void,
When released, it gleams.

Diane Stanley is the not-so-mysterious author and illustrator of many award-winning books for young readers. Her novels include BELLA AT MIDNIGHT, a *School Library Journal* Best Book of the Year and an ALA *Booklist* Editor's Choice; and THE MYSTERIOUS MATTER OF I. M. FINE, which also features Franny and Beamer. Well known as the author and illustrator of award-winning picture-book biographies, she is the recipient of the Orbis Pictus Award for Outstanding Nonfiction for Children and the *Washington Post*–Children's Book Guild Nonfiction Award for the body of her work.

Ms. Stanley has also written and illustrated numerous picture books, including three creatively reimagined fairy tales: THE GIANT AND THE BEANSTALK, GOLDIE AND THE THREE BEARS, and RUMPELSTILTSKIN'S DAUGHTER. She lives in Santa Fe, New Mexico. You can visit her online at www.dianestanley.com.